FICTION

M000100519

INQUIRIES & ADVERTISING

Address: Suite 22, 509 Commissioners Road West, London, Ontario, N6J 1Y5

Advertising: Email info@mysterymagazine.ca

Editor: Kerry Carter **Publisher:** Chuck Carter **Cover Artist:** Robin Grenville Evans

Submissions: https://mysterymagazine.ca/submit.asp

Mystery Magazine is published monthly by AM Marketing Strategies.

GREAT DAY TO BE ALIVE

Brigitte N. McCray

Some people will hug a person they haven't seen in a decade, like it's only been three days since they've seen them. Not the people in my hometown. I've spent the last decade in New York, a place they believe smells of piss and garbage, despite never having stepped foot in the city. They wouldn't dare leave the mountains of West Virginia.

I'm tainted by association.

And I'm an actress, which makes it worse.

"What TV show do I know you from, girl?" Terry Buchanan asks me in the Mountain Laurel Convenience Store and Deli.

God, I can't believe it's him. He has that Mountaineers baseball cap Daddy bought him for his seventeenth birthday. It's all dirty and stained now. He even has the same smirk and still stinks of Calvin Klein's CK One.

"Girl"? I'm nearing forty. Plus, he knows my damn name. We dated all four years of high school.

I'm in line holding an egg and cheese biscuit and a bottle of chocolate milk. "I know you remember my name, Terry."

He's standing behind me, all gruff and bearded. He's still slender, and instead of the football jersey he used to wear, he's in a car mechanic shirt. He's holding a newspaper under his arm. "Oh, I'm sorry, Patsy," he says. "Is 'girl' one of those words I'm no longer allowed to say, according to the politically correct police?"

I roll my eyes and place my food on the counter.

Candace Hopkins, cashier and owner, snorts. "I bet you're glad you didn't marry him." She didn't remember me last Tuesday, the day after I moved Mama into the nursing home. I've been here the last week clearing out the old house, and now every morning Candace nods and says, "Great day to be alive," just like she used to all those years ago when I'd come in for pop rocks and cherry soda. Her hair's grey now and she has fine lines around her mouth and eyes from smoking too many menthol cigarettes, the smell sticking to her clothes, but she's the same Candace.

The whole town is the same.

I'd be, too, if I had stayed and married Terry.

"Hey," he says, like he can't think of a single reason why a woman wouldn't marry him. I don't see a wedding ring, so I'm assuming he's still single. Join the club. If I did have someone, it'd make staying here for the next two weeks tolerable.

Candace hands me my receipt, and I scoop the items back into my arms, but Terry steps in front of the door. He sips from his steaming Styrofoam cup of coffee. Jesus, I miss my coffeeshop in Queens. I tried Candace's coffee, and I don't think my stomach lining has recovered.

"I remember now. One of those *Law & Order* shows," Terry says.

"*F.B.I.*," I say. I've done both, and plenty others, but *F.B.I.* is the most recent. I've been typecast as "victim #1." Or, "Jane Doe," until the detectives learn my character's name. I get to do a little acting before I'm killed in the first few minutes. Sometimes I do what we call "corpse duty." It's easy money in the bank.

I wave for him to move.

Terry steps back, saying, "You're good. Always were though."

"Thanks," I say. I had one short scene where I liked the way I made my body go slack and dropped the phone after a murderer slit my throat.

Even though he tried to convince me to stay after senior year, Terry was always my biggest cheerleader. At the curtain calls for the high school plays, he'd be the only student giving a standing ovation while hooting and hollering. I know it's pathetic, but I miss that kind of validation. In New York, nobody's impressed by the number of times you've played a corpse.

"I always knew you'd make it. Acting is what you always wanted. I'm glad someone got out of this town and did something to make us proud."

He always knew how to make me feel confident, like I was somebody who mattered.

"Speaking of crime," Candace says, "Be careful up at your house."

"Why?"

Terry spreads his newspaper out on the counter and points to the front page. CONVICTS ESCAPE, the headline reads.

"Near here?" I ask.

"They were transporting them from the jail to the state prison in a van, and the idiot guards left the inmates alone and went inside a Hardee's to eat. They were handcuffed in the van. Picked the locks though," Terry says, shaking his head.

I peer down at the paper and read more. "It was in Shelby. Ten miles away from us."

"They'll hide in the woods. It's the only place they'll be able to stay clear of all the road blocks and police," Candace says, as if she knows the criminal mind. I know it better from all those scripts I've read.

"Aren't the cops searching the woods?" I ask.

"Yeah. But close to that pig farm on Route 27. I'm betting they ran in the other direction, right towards us."

"Here?"

"Hard to say," Terry says. "Want me to come and check on you?"

Slick, just like in high school.

I laugh. "Come on. Y'all are just trying to scare me."

"Two murderers and a rapist. We all should be scared," Candace says.

"I'll be fine," I say, thinking about how secluded it is up on the mountain surrounded by all those woods at Mama and Daddy's house. It would be the perfect setting for one of those crime TV shows. I shake it off, trying to convince myself more than them, "I've got Daddy's rifle." It's somewhere in the house, but I worry I don't remember how to shoot. It's been a decade and a half since I've held a gun.

When Daddy taught me how to shoot, he said, "Now, I don't want you acting like one of those mountain women who chew tobacco and shoot for fun, but it's still important for you to know how to use one. Just in case. For protection." Women weren't supposed to be tough, unless they had to protect themselves.

"I'll come up there later and check on you anyway. We take care of each other in this town." Terry hands Candace his money.

"I remember." I push open the door with my back.

"Best part of this town."

"I guess." He's right. It is.

"Be careful," I say. "I just might shoot you." But I give him a wink.

Candace is the one who rolls her eyes this time.

After I eat my biscuits and down my chocolate milk, I start on the piles. I have three going. One for items to keep. I still need to rent a storage container. That goes on my list for tomorrow. Another pile for items to take to Goodwill. The third is for items I'm not sure about. I'll have to ask Mama or just figure it out myself. It's strange going through their belongings and making choices they can't. After Daddy died, I asked Mama every night on the phone if she needed help. Stubborn and strong, that woman. I didn't know about her dementia until her preacher called me after a visit. Maybe I didn't want to know. If I did, I would have visited before now, right? But I couldn't stand the thought of her needing help. Mama and Daddy were the strong ones. It's probably why I was so good at playing the role of the victim.

Around supper time, I flinch at a knock on the door.

Terry stands there with a box of pizza. "I'm guessing there's nothing in your fridge."

"Yeah," I say after a moment and let him in, although I'm grateful because I'm worn out from sorting.

"Boy, nothing much has changed," he says, standing in the middle of the living room and staring. "Just a bit messier."

"Yeah, it would kill Mama if she saw the house looking like this." Piles on the floor, the trash nearly overflowing, and half-packed boxes on the furniture.

"I pass the driveway every morning. It's been years, but I still feel like I should turn so I can pick you up for school. It's going to be strange to think of this house all empty." He places the pizza on the counter and takes out a slice. As he eats he wanders around to examine the photos I have left to pack.

It's extra cheese, what I always made him order in high school even though he preferred pepperoni, and I help myself to a slice. I relax on the couch. All these years, and I still feel comfortable around him. It's why I left right after high school. I knew if I stayed here with Daddy and Terry, I'd always be a shadow and never learn how to take care of myself. I've lived alone so long that it feels nice and easy to sit here with him, but I'm not missing my empty closet-sized apartment with moldy take-out in the fridge.

Eventually he sits next to me, and we eat two more slices together in silence before he says, "I've missed you."

The unexpectedness of the statement causes me to drop half the pizza on my shirt, but what's even more unexpected is that I lean over and kiss him. Damn, he's always been bad for me. I'd be performing in community theatre or regional theatre if he'd had his way. But what the hell else is there to do in this town right now? We're sixteen again, just like that, all tossing clothes and fumbling.

Afterwards, we're both awkward. We're our forty something selves again who haven't seen each other in years, all hiding our nakedness with our clothes and stumbling as we say goodbye. Before he leaves, he says he'll check on me in the morning, and once the door closes, I'm wondering why I didn't ask him to stay.

I stand there half-naked against the door. The sounds coming from the woods—an owl hooting, crunching scuffles—make me feel more alone and afraid, and I hate it, feeling weak again, like the last few years in New York have never happened.

I can't sleep. I toss and turn in the bed, staring at the clock and listening for the convicts out in the woods.

They don't come.

I miss the sounds of hogs rummaging in the woods. Daddy liked his hogs to roam the mountain so they could fatten up on acorns and chestnuts. It sweetened the meat. He built his slaughtering shed close to where the hogs liked to roam the most. It was easier that way—he didn't have to drag the hogs back to the house. I can't remember the last time he killed a hog. Years ago.

I eventually fall asleep for a couple of hours and dream of bloody hogs. When I wake up, it's a little after eight, and I know from seeing Terry at Mountain Laurel yesterday that he's supposed to be at work by that time. He hasn't come by like he said he would. It burns me up. If he wanted a one night's stand for old time's sake he could have just said so. I wouldn't have minded, but I could be dead in the house, the escaped convicts having killed me. How long would it be before someone thought to check on me?

I slam out of the house and speed down the dirt driveway. I can't wait to give him a piece of my mind, but I'm hungry, and I almost stop for breakfast so I can hear Candace say, "Great day to be alive." I drive by. I imagine the horn is Terry's head, and I lay down on it hard so she'll look out and see my car. With escaped convicts on the loose, it's important for everybody to know who's still kicking.

I drive by the garage, but his car isn't there.

Mama told me a couple of years ago that his Mama and Daddy died a year apart from cancer. The little light green shack still looks like it belongs to his parents. His mama's flowers are blooming and his daddy's porch swing moves gently in the morning spring breeze. The house sits next to the railroad tracks on the far side of town near the high school stadium. At night, we used to walk the tracks for a mile or two and then back to the stadium, where we'd sit smoking cigarettes and pot under the bleachers.

I've been stood up by men before in the City. Something about the history I share with Terry makes it worse.

I bang on his front door. There's no answer. Voices mumble inside. Something crashes. If there's a woman in there with him I really will punch him. "Terry?" I bang again, louder.

Two or three minutes pass. Finally, the lock unlatches and the door slowly opens a crack. I can just see a sliver of his face. He says, "I told you last night that I'd see you later. I'll meet you when I said I would."

I start to explain that he's confused or has his times mixed up. Then I think about how much like a scene from a movie or TV show this is, and I know what's keeping Terry from opening that door wider.

He shuts the door, and I'm standing on his porch, his Mama's "welcome" mat under my shoes, and I want to laugh at that and tell those three convicts that she didn't mean they were welcome at all. I shake it off. I need to call the police. My phone's in the car, and I've never played this role before, the part of a savior, and I'm not sure I know how to act it.

I take two steps towards the car.

The door creaks open.

I turn.

There's a gun pointed at me.

This is a role I know how to play.

I hold up my hands.

The man pointing the gun is a silver fox, his hair cut short, but wavy, a tiny ocean sitting on top of his head. He has a bit of beard stubble, and it's clear that he's used to a clean shave because he's rubbing at the stubble with his other hand. His skin looks like leather. He squints down at me and I wonder if he needs glasses. If this was a script, I'd write something in the margins about this character like, "Vain. Afraid of aging. Uses tanning bed regularly."

He waves me inside with the gun.

I enter, keeping my hands in the air. Passing him, I get a better look at the gun, a revolver, probably one Terry's Daddy used to keep for protection in the bedside table. The only time it'd ever been shot was when Terry took me out to the woods and taught me how. Daddy had already taught me though, and, just to make Terry feel all manly, I missed every bottle. Once he gave me some pointers, I started to nail the bottles, like he'd taught me something useful, even though I was a good shot already.

Drawers have been flung out on the floor. Clothes and papers lay scattered. Terry's mama had been neat as a pin, everything in her house put inside cabinets and cupboards. The floor had always been swept and mopped daily. Terry would have kept it up. He would have been too afraid she'd come back and haunt him if he didn't. So, I knew the convicts had made the disaster inside the house.

Terry's sitting straight on the couch with his hands under his ass, just like he did that time he came over to meet Daddy for the first time. Three orange jumpsuits lay crumbled on the floor. The man holding the gun wears a Mötley Crüe tee shirt. He's larger than Terry, and the tee stretches against his chest. The jeans, too, are snug, the cuffs hitting right at his ankles. He's still in his jail slippers. Terry's shoes must not have fit.

The other two sit in the living room. One rocking back and forth in Terry's mama's rocking chair. He's holding his stomach. He looks to be about twenty, and he's much smaller than Terry so that Terry's clothes, another tee shirt, but one so faded I can't tell what's on it, and another pair of jeans, practically swallow him.

The man places the gun against my back and pushes me towards Terry. "Sit," he commands, and I do, but then he points the gun at the young convict and says, "If you don't knock off that rocking I'm going to blow your fucking brains out of your head."

Twenty Something stops and clutches his stomach tighter.

The other convict, sitting in front of us in the recliner, has tried to disguise himself in some of Terry's mama's clothes. A flowered, southern church dress that fits like a tent. He has one of her Easter hats, wide brimmed and too many silk flowers, on his head.

"Donnie," Silver Fox says, "Take that shit off. This ain't no game."

"Why didn't you run?" Terry whisper-hisses when I sit beside him on the couch.

"There was no time," I whisper-hiss.

The man named Donnie throws the Easter hat on the coffee table. "The less we look like ourselves the better, right?"

"Now, we're going to ask you again," Silver Fox says to Terry. "Where's your money?"

"I told you," he says. "I don't have any cash around. All I have is in the bank."

Donnie slips Terry's mama's dress off. He's naked there in the living room. He's skinny, all ribs and muscle. He winks at me and kisses at me. I turn so I won't have to look at him. Terry removes his hands from under his ass and takes one of my hands. He squeezes, and I imagine him jumping up, grabbing the gun, and shooting them all.

"Here's what you're going to do," Donnie tells Terry. I hear him shaking out clothes, and I hope he's putting some on. "You're going to go to the bank and withdraw some cash. You won't alert the police because we've got your girl here. You wouldn't want anything to happen to her, would you?"

"Girl," again. If I wasn't so scared I'd jump up and slap that Donnie.

I've been here before, in some iteration or other. In every scene I've been in, the guy gets shot after the villains get what they want. My character's shot after that.

Silver Fox slaps Donnie on the side of the head.

"Fuck," Donnie says, knocking Silver Fox's hand away as it starts to come down with another blow.

"As soon as we release him he'll go and get help. Don't be so damn stupid."

"I won't tell," Terry says anxiously. "Don't hurt her. I'll go get some money from the bank."

Silver Fox points the gun at Terry. "Shut up."

Twenty Something sneezes and starts rocking again. Silver Fox points the gun at him and says, "What the hell did I tell you?"

He stops the rocking but says, "I should just turn myself in. Y'all leave me here. My stretch wasn't going to be that long anyway. Stupid to just run off like that."

Silver Fox ushers Donnie to follow him. They pass the couch to get to the kitchen. They're in there whispering.

Terry leans over to Twenty Something. "Call the cops. Turn yourself in and help us."

Before he can answer, Silver Fox and Donnie stroll back into the living room. I already know what's coming as soon as Silver Fox lifts the gun. I yank Terry out of the way.

Twenty Something gasps and jumps from the rocking chair, but that one shot is too quick. Pop! He slumps in the chair.

I cover my ears to try and stop the rattling in my eardrums. Terry does the same.

Twenty Something's shirt has a hole in it, and it's bloody and charred from the bullet. The smell of gun powder stings my nose. Terry won't be able to keep that rocker. The back is a mess, and the room stinks of shit.

"Sick and tired of all that rocking," Silver Fox says. "I told you it was useless to bring him along."

"I figured his parents would have some money," Donnie says. "I didn't think about the cops tapping our family phones."

Terry's shaking and muttering, "Dear God. God help us."

TV and film guns sound real. The fake blood they use looks real. I'm still surprised how calm I am.

I'm sick of playing a victim. God isn't going to help us, but I can.

"I've got some cash up at my house. You can have it and my car if you let us live."

Terry looks at me like he's thinking, "Are you crazy?"

I'm thinking I remember where Daddy stored his rifle.

As I drive through town, Terry's stuck in the backseat with Donnie, whose legs are too long for the Ford Fiesta I rented at Yeager Airport last week. Donnie keeps shifting in the seat and bumping Silver Fox's passenger seat. Silver Fox has the gun pointed at my side, but he rotates it to the rear and says, "If you hit my seat one more time, you're going to wind up like College Boy back there."

Donnie mumbles "sorry" and turns so that his knees point to Terry.

It seems like Silver Fox and Donnie met by chance on that jail bus, and, although Donnie's followed him, he's scared of Silver Fox. Not that I admire a murderer or anything, but I'm a bit in awe of a man who can take control after so little time, and I start wondering what he does for a living. I'm guessing a drug dealer or leader of some mountain mafia group. Both.

When we pass Candace's store, I slow the car down and put my hand on the horn, ready to blow it, but Silver Fox presses the gun into my side, saying, "Don't even think about it."

At Mama and Daddy's house, Silver Fox keeps the gun on me. Donnie pushes Terry up the porch. We follow. When I unlock the door, Donnie asks Silver Fox, "Where you think we should go? Mexico?"

"Canada is closer, you idiot."

"It gets cold there."

"I'd rather be cold than in prison."

Now in the hallway, I start towards the living room closet to grab the rifle, praying that Daddy left bullets in it and that it doesn't jam, but Silver Fox says, "Not so fast." He holds my arm. "You tell me where the money is, and I'll get it."

He's smart, that Silver Fox.

I consider what every movie and TV show like this depicts. In my first TV role, my character was killed and then the villain searched the house for money. She didn't have any time to defend herself. At least I'm still alive. In the show *Law or Justice*, my character told the villain where the money was and while he was searching for it, she got her gun, but the villain heard her and shot her first. So, I decide to do the opposite.

I don't have any cash anyway, so I say, "I lied." I tighten the elastic on my long ponytail and look around the house, considering my options. I step closer to Donnie and Terry.

"What do you mean?" Donnie shouts.

"You don't have any money here." Silver Fox smiles, like he's impressed and he moves closer.

Terry takes one step forward so he's standing beside me.

"Not in the house, no."

"Why'd you bring us here?" Donnie seizes the end of my ponytail. My scalp aches, but I ignore it. My hair's long enough that I twist behind Donnie. I tell Terry, "Push," and we both shove him towards Silver Fox. A few hair strands go with Donnie. The two men collide. I trip Donnie. They're a mess of limbs on the floor. Silver Fox still keeps hold of his gun. It gives me time though. I race to the closet and try to not think about my screaming scalp. The rifle's propped against the wall. I yank it out. I release the safety, thinking, "God, I hope I'm still a good shot," and I point it at the two men.

"Shit," Donnie squeals and fast crawls behind the sofa.

Terry runs to the kitchen.

Silver Fox aims his gun, and I drop. There's the deafening sound of his bullet, and it pierces the wall.

Fuck, now I'll have to fix the wall. I aim at him again, but he races left to the dining room. This at least gives me time to run to the kitchen, where Terry's huddled in front of the fridge.

I say, "Run and get help."

"Car?" he asks.

"Keys are out there with them. You'll have to run fast."

"I'm not as fast as I was in high school." What a stupid thing to say. He must be in shock.

"Just run," I say, and he's out of the back door with a bullet chasing him. It misses.

"Two against one, bitch," Donnie says, and I hear shoes running and suddenly he's in the kitchen with me, shouting behind him, "Come help me, Ken!"

When I pull the trigger, all I think is that Silver Fox's name can't be Ken. The name's too boring. In a script, he'd be Silver Fox.

Donnie looks down at his bloody stomach. "You shot me," he says, like he's surprised a woman is fighting back. He stumbles and hits his head on the marble counter before he falls to the ugly linoleum floor. It's a good thing I plan on replacing it before I sell.

I half expect Donnie to get up, hop around excitedly, and ask if we should do the scene again. Part of me wishes he would because I don't want to be responsible for taking his life, but another part of me thinks about the way he winked at me when he was naked. I don't need much of an imagination to know what kind of terror he inflicted on women.

"I like you," Silver Fox says from the living room. I can't see him, and I'm too worried about his gun to leave the kitchen.

"Why?" I ask, curious.

"You remind me of my daughter. She's tough, too."

I've never been called tough.

"She's overseeing my business right now. We could use someone like you. If we put our guns away and talk about this, I bet we can work something out."

Bullshit. He just wants me to come out so he can shoot me.

"I'm an actress."

He laughs.

This pisses me off.

I exit the kitchen shooting.

He dodges the bullets as he runs out of the front door.

I follow.

He heads to the woods, and I chase.

Terry will have the police here soon.

Daddy once shot a bear during his Thanksgiving Day hunt. When he returned, I cried. I was sixteen, but that bear in his pickup bed had all its power and strength sucked out. The only way Daddy calmed me was by saying, "It was do or die. That bear was rushing towards me. If I hadn't shot, I'd been bear meat."

Hunt or be the victim. Those are the only two options until the state police or town police get here.

The thing about the woods behind my house is that they lead all the way up the mountain. You can see Pennsylvania from the top. Silver Fox seems too old to run the five miles straight up. The forest has plenty of bushes to hide along the way.

I take cover behind a thick maple and scan the shades of green for his silver, wavy head. I glance behind me, wondering if I have it all wrong, that I'm the one being hunted, not the other way around. I see nothing and almost let out a long sigh of relief, but I gulp it down.

The only noises are some cliff swallows squeaking, and I relax.

The birds quiet. Something snaps, a branch or a twig, and leaves rustle. He pops out from behind a bush. He's rushing for me. I start to run, but he grabs me and wraps his arms tightly around my chest, saying, "Nobody shoots at me, damn it."

He leans and we both crash to the ground. My rifle falls to my side. I cough out a breath. My whole body feels like a car has hit me. He's on top of me, and if I can reach my rifle, maybe I can push him off me and use the butt to hit him in the gut, but his grip is too tight—his hands around my neck now. Where's his gun? In his pants? I don't care. I just want mine. And I reach it. He releases my neck just so he can peel my hands from the rifle, and he takes it.

Now he has two guns.

I know this game from one TV script. He's decided to play with me before he kills me.

I push him off me and use my knee to punch him in the gut.

I flee. He nearly catches my ankle, but I shake his hand loose.

I remember Daddy's hog slaughtering shed. I hope he left some tools I could use to defend myself. It's a mile away, and I'm fast. Unlike Terry, I'm actually faster than I was in high school. Nobody cared that much about exercise back then, but, corpse duty or not, I'm an actress and have to stay fit.

I hear Silver Fox's breathing. Despite his age, he must not be too far behind.

Soon, I'm in a clearing. I stop right before the hole in the ground that Daddy filled with water and heated rocks. I couldn't stand that part, the hog boiled to loosen the hair.

I rush to cover it with dead leaves, a hole I hope a new pig will fall into. A terrible part of myself wishes I could boil the hair off of Silver Fox's leather-like skin.

I run to the shed. Inside, there's the butcher's knife Daddy used to gut the hogs laying on the old table.

I hear a loud thud and leaves and dirt falling. Silver Fox shouts, "Fuck." I peek through a crack in the shed. The hole's tripped him. The rifle's been flung a few feet. He's dropped his revolver. He tries to push himself out of the hold, but he holds his hand, moaning, like his wrist is broken.

He pushes himself forward with one hand. His feet or legs must be hurt too badly from the hole.

I have to take the chance.

Holding the knife, I race for the rifle, but he uses his elbow, moving himself faster, and we reach it at the same time. Gun or knife? I pick the rifle and throw the knife behind me, making sure it lands close enough in case I need it.

He pushes himself to his knees, and we yank the rifle back and forth. I shove him hard. He shrieks in pain, falling to his side, but he manages to grab the rifle as he falls. I was too confident I had the rifle, my grip too loose. I take hold of it and pull. I get it. I aim at him.

Why isn't he pulling out his gun? I don't shoot because it doesn't seem fair. How many rounds does his revolver have? Maybe ten? I'm guessing he's out of bullets. He lets out a defeated laugh, unable to move.

Shouts in the distance. Footsteps rushing through the woods.

It's over. I've won. I drop the rifle to the ground.

That's not enough.

I grab the knife instead.

I know that look he gives me. I've used it for every victim #1 or Jane Doe character I've ever played. The look right before the killer makes the character a victim.

I thrust the knife inside Silver Fox's belly, just like Daddy taught me to do during hog slaughtering season. All those years in the City working to rid myself of my roots, my accent, but I'm a woman who knows how to shoot a gun and kill a hog.

A woman who's tough.

About twenty police officers rush in and surround Silver Fox. They tell me to drop the knife and put my hands in the air. Someone takes the knife and they bag it.

A little while later, I'm sitting on the back of an ambulance, and Candace comes up beside me. Terry's on my other side, and I feel his arm wrap around me.

She says, "Great day to be alive."

I turn and kiss Terry hard.

I pull away and walk towards the officers to give them my statement, where I'll play the victim one final time.

MURDER, MY SUITE

John H. Dromey

Strictly speaking, I was not *in* bed when the persistent jangle of a telephone woke me from a dreamless sleep. I was lying fully-clothed *on* a comfy bed in a fancy hotel.

Maybe Pinkerton agents never sleep, but I do. Any chance I get. Even so, I can't ever seem to get enough rest to make up for the long hours of alertness my job sometimes requires.

The phone continued to ring. I wiped some of the sleep from my eyes before I reached for the receiver.

"Murphy," I said. My voice was more of a savage growl than intelligible human speech.

The man on the other end of the line wasn't fooled for even a minute into thinking the switchboard operator had connected him with the zoo.

"It's time, Séamus," the hotel manager said. By the way, it's pure coincidence my given name is pronounced the same as a slang term for my profession—shamus.

I cleared my throat. "Time for what?" I asked.

"You know what. Now, quit stalling. Get your keester up to the penthouse pronto."

Propping myself up on one elbow, I fumbled the handset back into its cradle on the second try.

Still a bit groggy, I swung my legs off the bed and walked over to the hand basin. I splashed some cold water in my face and ran my wet fingers through my hair.

Fully awake, I was ready for work. I'd slept in my clothes to save time. All I had to do was slip into my trench coat and grab my hat. Lucky for me, I didn't have far to go. My assignment was at the top of the building and I was only one floor below. Given my druthers, I'd go out of my way to avoid situations that are over my head, but this time I had no choice.

As soon as I stepped out of the room, I could hear the elevator ascending. I went to the stairwell and took the steps two at a time.

I was in place, leaning against the wall next to the main entrance to the penthouse suite when two men stepped into the hallway.

It was a mere formality, but the elevator operator stuck his head out of the iron cage long enough to see if anyone was waiting to go back down. He did a double take when he saw me. I waved my hand like I was shooing a fly, and the vertical trolley conductor withdrew his head fast enough to make a turtle jealous. He probably knew, or suspected, where I go, trouble follows, or vice versa.

The two gents approaching me were a study in contrasts. One had an obvious abundance of muscles and didn't appear to have a care in the world. The other was pintsized, and—if I'm any judge of character—despite his wooden expression was about as nervous as a rocking chair in a room full of termites.

I opened the door with a passkey and ushered the disparate duo into the swanky interior.

I didn't waste any time or words. With my footsteps muffled by a thick carpet, I led the way to an interior door. Looking back to see if the other two had followed, I lightly bumped by knuckles against the highly polished wood a couple of times before I got a firm grip on the silver-plated handle. I turned the knob and stepped aside as the door swung open.

With a quick intake of breath, the wiry fellow stepped right up to the threshold. I started to put out a restraining hand, but he just stood there staring.

There was plenty to see.

A big man, bent at the waist, was standing on the far side of a four-poster bed. Perhaps tipped off by my earlier clumsiness, he was aware he had company. The man straightened up slowly and gave us a disapproving look. He was holding a coil of rope. Almost as an afterthought, he switched the convoluted cord from one hand to the other and then held it behind his back. Out of sight, but not out of mind.

Even so, he was not the center of attention for long. That role was assumed by the shapely female form stretched out—motionless—on top of the chenille bedspread. Her long tresses obscured much of her face, but her neck was bare. There were angry red marks on her throat.

"What do you think?" I asked the short man.

"I think she got what she deserved," he said.

My heart skipped a beat. I reached in front of the little fellow and quickly pulled the door closed.

"Did you recognize her?" That was the sixty-four-dollar question. I held my breath while I waited for an answer.

"No, but I've seen my share of two-bit floozies," he said in a flat voice completely devoid of emotion.

That made my job a whole lot easier. As long as I didn't have good cause to feel sorry for the guy, what came next would go much smoother. I took a firm grip on his nearest arm and guided him toward a writing desk nestled in a corner of the room.

"I was told you're mighty handy with a pen," I said.

He tensed up a bit, but kept walking. "So, what if I am?"

I pointed to the top of the desk where a blank sheet of paper, a fountain pen, and an ink blotter were laid out. "You can put your skills to work writing a farewell note for the occupant of the adjoining room."

"Saying what?"

"The usual stuff, but keep it short and simple. 'Good-bye cruel world' or 'I can't live with the guilt.' Use your imagination."

He shook his head. "It won't work. Even if I knew what name to sign, I can't forge a signature without seeing a copy of her handwriting."

"Quit dragging your feet," I told him. "You don't need to know her name any more than you need to know the names of the other people involved in this sordid affair. Your job and mine is to protect the reputation of somebody whose name you'd probably recognize, but you won't hear it from me. Like it or not, your cooperation is vital."

"What if I refuse?"

"If you prefer, you can join our guest in the bedroom." I opened the top of my coat to reveal my shoulder holster was occupied by a .38. "The muscle-bound gent in there has a gun as well as a rope. He can arrange the crime scene so the police will deduce a lovers' quarrel prompted a strangulation followed by remorse and a self-inflicted gunshot. I suggest you write the note and leave it unsigned."

The pipsqueak caved. He picked up the pen, leaned over the desk, and scribbled a few lines. His hand wobbled a bit as he wrote, and—whether intentional or not—that added a nice touch to the document.

"Are we done here?" he asked.

"Just about," I said. "Come with me. We need to have a private talk."

I moved slowly toward the outside door. The little guy followed me like a lamb to the slaughter. I glanced back once to make sure the big guy was keeping his distance. He was.

I edged to one side and moved closer to the admitted forger so I could speak to him without raising my voice, but also to block his view of the room.

I explained briefly how I thought he should spend the rest of the evening hiding out in a hotel a few blocks away. I gave him directions.

"You can't take a taxi. That would leave a trail. On the other hand, it isn't safe for someone like you to be out on the streets by yourself at this time of night." I crooked my left arm in front of my chest and pointed my index finger toward the inside of the penthouse. "If you agree to go to a rival flophouse, you're welcome to take that pair of bruisers along as bodyguards."

The paperhanger gave a brief nod. He'd taken the bait.

I pulled a couple of ten-dollar bills out of my shirt pocket.

"One of these is for your trouble. When you get to the hotel, slip the other sawbuck to the night clerk and he'll let you sign the register with a fake name and a phony time of arrival. That will give you a solid alibi in the unlikely event you need one."

I looked back toward the bedroom. The outside man caught my eye just before he opened the door and the inside man stepped out.

"Make sure our colleague gets to where he's going in one piece," I told them. "He knows the way."

The trio left without saying another word. The door clicked shut behind them. I hurried across the room and looked at the escritoire. The note was gone. There was nothing I could do about that. I put the ink pen and blotter in a drawer.

Looking for any other loose ends to tidy up, my next stop was the bedroom. The body did not appear to have been moved. The coil of rope was in plain sight at the foot of the bed where it had been tossed.

There was no time to enjoy the scenery.

"Wake up, Sleeping Beauty," I said to the negligee-clad doll in the four-poster. "We need to get out of here before the maids make their rounds."

Nothing.

I slapped her on her barely-covered bottom. That got her attention.

"Cut that out, buster! I'm not being paid enough for you to take liberties."

"Yeah? Well, unless you take it on the lam pronto, you may not have any liberty at all."

She sat up. "What do you mean?"

"If the wrong people find out you participated in this little escapade, you could go to jail or wind up in the morgue for real."

"I don't believe you. Making motion pictures is not against the law. Besides, this was just a rehearsal. By the way, how did I do?"

"I'm no expert, but I'll wager you violated the Hays Code six ways to Sunday."

"Huh?"

"If you'd revealed any more of your gams, the mark might not have noticed your face at all."

"That was the idea, according to the goon you hired."

"Let me set you straight, sister. I'm not the moneybags of this operation."

"Who is?"

"I don't know and I wouldn't tell you if I did. I do know it's time to scram. Now, you can leave willingly, or I can drag you out of here kicking and screaming. It's your choice."

"Where are my clothes?"

"Your suitcase is in my room one floor down."

"I can't take the elevator dressed like this," she said.

"You won't have to. I'll loan you my coat and we'll take the stairs. This may come as a complete surprise to you, but you're about the most contrary dame I've ever met."

"My name is Marigold."

"Séamus." I picked up the rope from the bed. "Wrap this around your waist."

"Why?"

"We can't leave it here and I don't want anyone else to see it. Do this right and it will be concealed by my coat."

"That dirty old rope looks really scratchy. Why can't I just hold it in place with my arm?"

I was tired of arguing. I helped Marigold into my coat and pulled the strap nice and snug for her while she pressed the coiled rope to her side with her right arm. We got out of the penthouse suite and halfway to the stairwell before the rope slid to the floor. Rather than waste precious time undoing the coat and cinching it again, I picked up the rope and kept walking.

"I thought you wanted to keep that hidden?"

"I changed my mind," I said. "If somebody sees me, I'll pretend I'm a cowboy."

No one saw us.

As soon as we were inside the room, Marigold had me turn my back while she got dressed. All the while, she bombarded me with comments and questions.

"I can hardly wait to tell my girlfriends about my great adventure," she said. "If it wasn't for a motion picture, what was all the fuss about?"

I let out an audible sigh. It was decision time. Should I spin a fairy-tale, or tell Marigold the truth? I opted for the latter.

"I'm a little hazy on some of the details, but I'll tell you what I know. The bogus homicide was staged for the benefit of one person only. I don't know his name, but we can call him George. In addition to being a counterfeiter and a forger, George is a bookkeeper for a criminal mastermind."

"I heard what he said about me. He's not a nice person."

"I agree, but that's neither here nor there. By putting a scare into the accountant, we hoped to turn him into a stool pigeon."

"Who's 'we'?"

"You, me, and a couple of out-of-town coppers."

"How do you know they're cops?" Marigold asked. I thought there was a slight edge to her voice.

"I don't. I'm not for sure, but as far as I could tell, those two men were straight shooters and definitely on the right side of the law. I'm convinced of that even if we did blur the lines a bit between right and wrong with our unconventional methods."

"If the accountant becomes a police snitch, won't he be in danger? What's to prevent the mastermind from having George rubbed out?"

"That's where the second part of the scheme comes into play," I said.

"You haven't fully explained the first part," Marigold objected. "What's so scary about seeing a fake corpse? George seemed to take it in stride."

"He was not so sanguine about what followed. With an implied threat, I persuaded George to write a fake suicide note. That made him complicit in a crime. If he'd turned the paper over, he'd have seen it was stationery from the rival hotel which I recommended he go to in order to establish an alibi. Our two accomplices went with him. Do you understand the situation so far?"

By this time Marigold was fully clothed and we were speaking face-to-face. She nodded.

"If everything went according to plan, the two men escorted George to the roof of the hotel. Up there, they used the bookkeeper's wallet as an anchor to keep the suicide note he'd written from blowing away. At that point, George could either rat out his boss or become a fall guy. Stool pigeons can't fly. I hope he chose wisely."

"Are you suggesting they'd actually throw that poor soul off the roof if he failed to cooperate?

I dodged Marigold's question, as best I could "Do you have a radio?" I asked.

"No, I can't afford one."

"Do you read the newspaper?"

"Every day."

"Tomorrow then, look for a photo of a body found in an alley behind a hotel. If you find one, that's bad news. On the other hand, if the story is a brief item buried somewhere in the back pages of the newspaper without a photo, then you can deduce that George agreed to spill the beans, and for his protection our accomplices helped him fake his death."

"What difference does the lack of a photo make?"

"One chalk outline looks pretty much like another. A crime journalist worth his salt wouldn't waste film unless he can see an actual body in place. You successfully impersonated a corpse, but you only had to hold still for a few seconds. Can you imagine trying to pull off that same feat on cold, damp pavement?"

Marigold looked thoughtful, but didn't say anything.

Justice is supposed to be blind, but I'd gone into this situation with my eyes wide open. Now, I'd have to live with the consequences. Was I right to trust Marigold? I needed to know, or thought I did. I decided to ask her directly.

"Have I convinced you it's in the best interest of everyone involved for you to keep your trap shut?"

"In principle, I agree with you," she said. "But there is *one* person I need to tell."

My heart beat a little faster. I was hesitant to inquire further, but my peace of mind was at stake. Would she confide only in a trustworthy, tight-lipped acquaintance? I could only hope so. Otherwise, I might be losing sleep over this covert caper for a long time to come.

"Who's that?" I asked.

"My boss," Marigold said. "I'm a secretary for the chief of police. He'll be pleased to know his decision to hire a private eye to help out in this case was a good one."

PYTHAGORAS THE DOG IS MISSING

Jess Faraday

The first call buzzed in when I was eight feet up a lamppost with a pair of scissors Pet snatchers had settled into the neighborhood over the past few weeks, and they used arrangements of zip ties around lampposts and telephone poles to point the way to houses where people routinely left their dogs unattended. Snipping the ties on my way to my veterinary practice had become a daily ritual.

By the time I slid down the pole, my watch was humming like a hive of angry hornets. I took out my phone.

"Doc, where are you?" my intern, Tate, said when I picked up.

"Making life harder for our friendly neighborhood dognappers. What's up?"

"Well, it looks like they've brought the fight to us."

"You mean beyond graffiti and flaming cat poo on the doorstep?" Our attempts to raise awareness of the pet snatching problem had made us a few enemies.

"Someone broke into the kennels last night and they took Pythagoras."

The breath went out of me and my heart started to pound.

"Wait," I said, mentally scrolling through our current list of boarders. "Which one is Pythagoras?"

"You know, the Jack Russell who came in yesterday afternoon?"

I sighed. The dog's name was Jackie. I'd done the intake myself. "Tate, I told you, nicknaming the animals only makes things harder for the rest of us."

"It's not a nickname! Pythagoras the Counting Dog was in our boarding kennel, and now she's missing! Man, this is going to blow up the Internet."

"What? Did you put this online?"

A year ago Tate had nearly brought down my practice when he'd posted videos of my glow-in-the-dark rescue rabbit. The rabbit had glowed when she came to me, but it didn't stop legions of animal lovers from accusing me of dyeing her fur, injecting her with alien DNA, and worse. Tate had kept his snout clean since then, but when it came to broadcasting his business—and our clinic's business—to the digital world, sometimes he couldn't help himself.

"No, Doc, I swear. But everyone knows Pythagoras, and now she's been kidnapped. Just get down here!"

I wondered how much help the police would be. Pets were property under the law, and a recent voter measure had made theft or property damage of less than a thousand dollars in value a misdemeanor on par with a speeding ticket. As for the harassment of our clinic, I'd reported each incident dutifully, but the Sheriff's Department had maintained that they couldn't do much unless the perps either left a clue to their identity or committed a more serious crime.

Perhaps this attack on our facilities would be serious enough.

Cursing, I shoved the phone back into the pocket of my cargo pants and pointed my mountain bike into the Fairfax Avenue early traffic. As I pushed out into the street, a horn blared. I pulled back just in time to avoid being flattened by a black Suburban, but the dusty wind that followed it left me choking.

The San Vicente Veterinary Group was located in a converted ranch house on the northwestern fringe of West Hollywood. The vet from whom I'd purchased the practice had turned the carport into a set of indoor/outdoor dog kennels. By day the dogs could go back and forth between the indoor section of their runs and the outdoor section, which was backed by a chain link fence. At night the techs brought the dogs in and latched the separating doors from the inside.

Before I'd even rolled into the parking lot, I could see where someone had cut through the chain link back of the run farthest from the main building. As I drew closer, I saw that they had also kicked the wooden separating door to smithereens.

Poor Jackie. Jack Russells were high strung at the best of times. She must have been terrified.

"I've called the cops," Tate said as he ran down the back ramp to meet me. "They should be here any minute."

To my surprise, two sheriff's deputies arrived before I'd even locked my bike.

"Dr. Kulkarni," one of them called.

"Deputy Huerta."

At five foot four, Deputy Anna Huerta was taller and much more thoroughly muscled than me. She wore her jet-black hair pulled back tightly, her uniform sharply creased, and her shoes polished to a shine. Today she was accompanied by a male deputy who looked as if he could have been moonlighting as the lead of the superhero flick filming down the street.

"I hear you've had a break-in," Huerta said as I showed them in through the back door.

"Pythagoras the Counting Dog has been kidnapped from our kennels," Tate announced.

Huerta swivelled her head toward him. "And you are?"

"That's Tate Maxwell, my intern," I said. Huerta's partner, Addison, to go by the name on his shield, scribbled the information onto a notepad that looked comically small in his supersized mitt. "There has been a kidnapping, but the dog's name is Jackie. She's a Jack Russell Terrier."

"Who can do multiplication and division," Tate said.

"Long division?" Huerta asked.

"What's long division?"

"Before your time," I said.

"Anyway, she's a star. An Internet sensation."

"Is that why you think the dog was taken?" Addison asked me.

I said, "I think my intern is misinformed. We're talking about an ordinary pet who checked into our boarding kennel yesterday afternoon." I crossed to the wall of patient files, pulled the appropriate folder, and handed it to her. "Here's the paperwork. This morning the dog was gone, and it's clear that someone broke into the kennel to take her."

Huerta scanned the intake form then handed it off to her partner to copy down the relevant information. "I'd like to have a look at the kennels."

"Certainly," I said. I led the deputies down the hallway, past the examination rooms, to the kennel entrance. "It's the one at the very end. It should be unlocked."

"You don't believe me!" Tate accused once the deputies had passed by us.

I said, "I appreciate what you're trying to do, and it's not a bad thought. If the police think that Jackie's a celebrity, they'll probably put more effort into finding her. Eventually, though, they'll figure out that it's not true—"

"But it *is* true!"

He pulled out his phone and scrolled through the apps until he found one called Dog Tok. Its symbol was a derpy looking cartoon mutt with a flop of fur over its eyes and a lolling tongue. He fiddled with it for a moment then turned the device toward me, revealing a stream of videos and animations declaring *Pythagoras the Counting Dog is Missing*.

"News travels fast," I said. Too fast, considering we'd only just discovered the break-in. It couldn't be the same dog, unless ... "You sure you didn't blab about this online?"

"I swear." Tate traced an 'X' beneath his left shoulder. "Oh ... wow ... these videos were posted yesterday afternoon."

"But you think it's the same dog?"

"No question. Check this out. Here's Pythagoras." He showed me an older video of the Jack Russell in question, then his fingers tickled over the screen and he brought up a photo from his phone's photo gallery. "And *here's* Pythagoras."

"A lot of Jack Russells look very similar," I said.

"But how many have the empty set symbol on their bellies?" He brought up a photo of our boarder displaying a marking that looked strikingly like the mathematical symbol. "Now look at this." He flipped back to Dog Tok and found a video of the famous counting dog getting a tummy rub.

That did give me pause. The unusual markings weren't just similar; as far as I could see, they were exactly the same, and in exactly the same place.

"You don't see that every day," Huerta said, suddenly at my shoulder.

"You don't see that on any day," I said. "How long have you been standing there?"

"Long enough to hear that two identical dogs have gone missing from the same city in the space of two days."

"Not identical," I said. "I hate to admit it, but I think my intern is right. These have to be the same dog."

Footsteps sounded in the hallway as Addison came trotting up. "Someone really did a job on the separating door. Do you think it'll be expensive to replace?"

"Somewhere north of a thousand dollars, I'd imagine," I said. Huerta scowled, but I smiled sweetly. "Quality is everything."

Tate's phone jangled with a few tinny bars of electronic music. Huerta turned her laser eyes on him.

"Sorry," he said. "Just watching Pythagoras at work. She's really amazing."

Huerta said, "My kids showed me some of those videos a few weeks ago. May I?"

Tate handed over his phone. Pythagoras's owner was an influencer named Makayla Finney. Like a lot of the influencers I'd seen, she was in her twenties, tall and thin, with a waterfall of light blonde hair and enough perfectly airbrushed makeup to make me wonder how she could contort her face into all of those exaggerated smiles and pouts.

She wasn't smiling now, though.

"If you've seen Pythagoras, please contact me on Dog Tok, or at this number ..."

"This isn't the person who checked the dog into the kennel yesterday," I said.

"Jennifer Howard," Addison read from his little notepad.

"That's right."

Ms. Howard had been a middle-aged woman in jeans and river sandals. She'd had a cloud of unruly curls, and had made no attempt to color away the greys or spackle over the fine lines around her eyes and mouth. I doubted she would so much as think of popping her denim-clad booty for the camera.

Huerta's expression went hard. "Did you get Ms. Howard's contact information?" she asked Addison. Her partner held up his little notepad. "Right. I'm going to ask the both of you not to discuss this with Ms. Howard or anyone else until you hear from us. Oh, and you can fill out a report for the property damage online." She handed me a card with the contact information for the L.A. County Sheriff's Department, then turned on her heel, leaving Addison to follow.

Normally, when there's an incident with an animal, I let the owner know first thing. But Jackie and Pythagoras had to be the same dog, which meant that Jennifer Howard wasn't the owner. At the same time, she hadn't felt like a dognapper to me. Some people simply own pets, and others are animal people. Ms. Howard felt like animal people, and I had a difficult time believing that she'd deliberately harm a dog. On top of that, no one would check an animal into a boarding facility only to break in later and steal it.

A counting dog must be a hot commodity indeed.

I walked back to the kennel with a wastebasket and broom. Cleanup was Tate's job, but there weren't any appointments that morning, and I needed distraction. I started by picking up the larger pieces of the shattered separating door and putting them into the wastebasket. Then I swept the inside section of the kennel. I was ducking through the doorway of the outer section when my hand brushed against something on top of the outside door frame. I jerked my hand back, and it dropped to the pavement: a little plastic cow the size of my thumb. A child's toy.

My first thought was that one of the techs had given it to the Jack Russell to play with, but they all knew that something that size was a choking hazard. What's more, it hadn't been lying in the corner; it had been balanced on the door frame in the outdoor section. Someone had to have put it there deliberately. Frowning, I picked up the little cow and went back inside.

"You know anything about this?" I asked, showing the toy to Tate. He shook his head. "Someone set it on the outside frame of the dog door in the last kennel. The deputies must have missed it."

Tate shrugged. "You want me to go back and clean up the debris from the break-in?"

"I just did," I said. "But maybe you can tell me more about this whole counting dog business."

My training had included quite a bit of animal psychology. It came in handy when I had to trick a cat into taking a pill without taking one of my fingers with it. As far as I remembered, though, that training hadn't said anything about canine mathematical abilities. The dimmest Irish Setter can spot the difference between a larger pile of kibble and a smaller one. As far as I knew, though, not even a Jack Russell—second in intelligence only to a Border Collie—could tell you how many pieces were in both piles combined.

Tate showed me a handful of the 15-second videos of Pythagoras pawing the ground in response to various written arithmetic problems. While it all looked very impressive, I wasn't seeing anything that suggested more than some dedicated reward and reinforcement training.

"I don't get it," I said. "Either of us could do that with any of the dogs in the kennel, given enough time and enough treats."

Tate sighed. "Sorry, Doc. I forgot your generation does better with long form."

"My generation?"

He held up a patronizing finger then used the finger to tap and swipe at the screen, eventually bringing up a half-hour documentary on Pythagoras the Counting Dog.

"Half an hour is long form?" I said.

"Just watch it."

The program examined several claims of counting dogs. Many of them, as I suspected, turned out to have been trained to respond to specific visual or auditory clues, most commonly cards with the problems written on them. The trainers used the same cards every time, or asked the same questions using identical words and intonation.

Pythagoras really did seem to be different though. In her videos, Makayla Finney wrote the problems fresh every time, sometimes using a whiteboard and markers, sometimes a pen and paper, and sometimes typing the problems onto a computer screen. Part of the documentary took place in a school room, where Ms. Finney and Pythagoras had challenged a class of eight-year-olds to a speed math contest. In this segment, she hand wrote problems onto a digital whiteboard at the front of the classroom.

Not only did Pythagoras get the answers correct nine times out of ten; she was faster than the kids.

"All right," I admitted. "That is impressive."

"You see? A dog that smart has got to be worth a lot of money. No wonder someone took her."

"Twice," I said.

"Maybe the dognappers are escalating," Tate said. He watched a lot of true crime and peppered his vocabulary with words like 'escalating.'

"So Ms. Howard stole Pythagoras from Ms. Finney, and Johnny Dogsnatcher stole her from us?"

Tate shrugged. "Maybe."

"Maybe." I picked up the little cow. "But this strikes me as some sort of calling card. What do you think it means?"

Drop-ins started trickling into the practice about eleven, and by early afternoon we were slammed. A canine stomach bug was making the rounds, and judging by my waiting room, the streets of West Hollywood must have been flowing with doggy diarrhea. It wasn't all bad news, though. One of my patients dropped in to tell me that he'd recovered the Boxer mix that had disappeared from his back yard last week.

"Hikers found him wandering around in Fryman Canyon Park," he said.

"Fryman Canyon Park? How did he get all the way up there?" It wasn't the first time that dog had jumped the fence, but it seemed a long way to go for an outdoor adventure.

He shrugged. "I can't figure it out either, but I won't be leaving him in the backyard unsupervised again."

Ten minutes past closing, Tate was disinfecting the last examination room and I was filling out an order for more Pupto Bismol to replenish our stores, when the practice's phone rang.

"Dr. Kulkarni, it's Jennifer Howard. Please don't hang up. This is my one phone call."

"You stole Pythagoras the Counting Dog," I said.

There was a long pause, then she said, "Yes ... but ... not intentionally."

A day and a half earlier, Jennifer Howard had been leaving the dog park on San Vicente with her own dog, when she noticed a rustling in the bushes on one side of the fenced dog area. Soon, a little white head popped out of the foliage.

"Let me guess," I said. "It was Pythagoras."

"Only I didn't know it just then. I mean, everyone knows Pythagoras, but it wasn't until I saw her owner's hot pink Porsche that I made the connection."

"Why didn't you tell the owner that her dog was escaping?"

"It all happened so fast. Pythagoras dug out and came over to say 'hi' to my dog. She just jumped right into my passenger seat like she belonged there. Then I saw the Porsche, made the connection, and took off."

"But *why?*"

"Have you ever seen those videos, Dr. Kulkarni? A lot of times when you see dogs doing amazing tricks like that, you know they're being abused."

"That dog didn't look abused when you brought her in," I said. I volunteered my services with two different rescues, and I was intimately familiar with the signs of abuse and neglect. As for digging out of the dog park, many Jack Russells were accomplished escape artists and did it for fun.

"I know ... I panicked. I thought about going back to the dog park, but how would I explain having driven off with Pythagoras in my car in the first place? And the longer I drove around thinking about it, the worse it would seem when I did bring her back. And you know, Pythagoras looks calm in the videos, but in real life she's a little demon. I thought she'd tear my car apart."

"A real Jack Russell Terror," I said, borrowing the term from another Jack Russell owner I knew. If they weren't so cute, the breed would die out fast.

"Exactly. I couldn't bring her back to the park, but what was I supposed to do with her? If I brought her home, she'd probably have destroyed the place."

"So you decided to drop her off at my kennel."

"Only when I saw the Suburban."

"What Suburban?" My heart started to pound again as I remembered my close encounter that morning.

"There was a big, black Suburban in my rear-view mirror. It was following me, and they didn't seem to care if I knew. That's when I saw the sign for your boarding kennel. I pulled into the alley behind your clinic, and the Suburban kept going. After I calmed down, I thought it might be better for everyone if I left Pythagoras with you. Oh, Dr. Kulkarni, this is such a mess, but I swear I didn't mean any harm."

"I believe you, but I'm not sure there's anything I can do."

"When the police came, my dog was in my back yard, alone. Can you go pick her up? I'm worried with all the dognappings going on."

"Sure." I took down her address. "What kind of dog is she?"

"An Irish Setter. Her name is Sinead."

Of course it was. "Is she aggressive?" It was doubtful with that breed, but it never hurt to check.

"Nah, she's a marshmallow. She'll come right with you."

"Ok, fine." Then I thought of another way I could help. "Ms. Howard, do you have a lawyer?"

"No."

"If you like, I can call a friend of mine. I helped her out when her rottweiler ate a silk ballet slipper. She owes me one."

Jennifer Howard lived on a narrow back street of stucco cube houses with chain link enclosed yards. Her four-room scrambled-egg colored box sat on a bare dirt lot punctuated by derelict sprinkler heads. A gate to the right of the property marked the yard where Ms. Howard had said Sinead would be waiting.

My pulse picked up at the sight of a black Suburban parked in front of the place. As I pulled the clinic van behind it, the vehicle suddenly took off, a rust-colored Irish Setter face grinning at me through the back window.

"Oh, I don't think so," I said as I popped the van into gear.

Chasing after a dognapper, not to mention one who had nearly run me down that morning, was foolhardy at best, but when an animal is in danger, I latch on like a pit bull. As the vehicle careened north through the narrow streets, I followed as closely as the parked cars and bicycle traffic would allow. Eventually the Suburban turned onto Laurel Canyon Boulevard, which was, for once, not clogged with cars inching past the hill-clinging mansions. We sped past the Love Street House where Jim Morrison had lived, slowing just enough near the Canyon Country Store for me to wonder what I'd actually do if I caught the miscreant.

Fortunately—or not—I wouldn't have the chance to find out.

No sooner had the Suburban put on the gas for the uphill thrust into the hills than my vehicle was suddenly, inexplicably surrounded by sheep. I slammed on the brakes and my van squealed to a stop. Frantic knocking at the window made me jump.

"What do you think you're *doing?* Are you *trying* to murder my babies?"

The hippies had left Laurel Canyon a long time ago, but they'd apparently forgotten Little Bo Peep and her flock. Or perhaps her grandparents, I thought, given her youth. I wondered what kind of work a twenty-five-year-old could get that would pay for a house in the Canyon, rainbow-colored dreadlocks, a five-hundred-dollar silk Indian print maxi dress ... and sheep.

Noticing the *Vegan!* button on her straw hat, I flashed my membership card for the American Veterinarian Medical Society. "Sorry, ma'am," I said. "It's an animal emergency."

Her mouth made a little pink "o." She put two fingers in her mouth and whistled. To my amazement, the flock moved clear of my van, gathering around the shepherdess's bare feet like a dust-speckled cloud. As I eased the van forward, she leaned in to get a thumbs-up selfie with my startled face in the background. A few more finger flicks, and the image was no doubt on its way to her legions of followers.

By that time, of course, the Suburban had disappeared into the snake's nest of roads that tangled through the Hollywood Hills. I scowled at the shepherdess then pulled into the parking lot of the Country Store and whipped out my own phone.

"I need to speak to Deputy Huerta," I said.

"I'm sorry, ma'am. Deputy Huerta is in a meeting. Would you like to leave a message?"

Cursing, I clicked off. I glanced up the road toward the hills. The Suburban was long gone, and there was no way of knowing where in that Gordian knot of dirt roads and private driveways it might have gone. On the other hand, if I started back toward West Hollywood Station now, I might be able to catch Huerta coming out of her meeting.

No such luck, the desk sergeant informed me when I arrived, but I was welcome to wait. Sighing, I took a seat and flipped through a three-year-old issue of *Cop's Life*. Eventually the door opened, and a uniformed officer showed me through to Huerta's desk.

"Dr. Kulkarni," she said. "To what do I owe the pleasure?"

"I've just witnessed a kidnapping." Her eyes widened. "Of a dog." Her eyes narrowed. "A dog belonging to Jennifer Howard, whom you have in custody. I was her one phone call," I explained.

"Have a seat."

The wooden chair wasn't much softer than the plastic ones in the reception area, but at least it didn't feel like it would wobble out from under me. I explained how Ms. Howard had used her call to ask me to fetch her Irish Setter from her back yard.

"You're sure it was really her dog?" Huerta asked.

I blinked. "I didn't ask," I admitted. "I probably should have. But it doesn't matter. As I arrived, a black Suburban was pulling out with the Irish Setter inside."

"A black Suburban?" Was that a flicker of interest in Huerta's voice?

"When I spoke to her, Ms. Howard said she'd pulled into the alley behind my clinic because a black Suburban had been following her. I should probably also mention that a black Suburban nearly mowed me down on my bike this morning."

By this point, Addison had wandered over, along with a few other officers.

"There's also this," I said. I brought out the little plastic cow and set it on the desk in front of her.

"Where did that come from?" Now Huerta looked like a hound who had caught a scent.

"I found it on the frame of the doorway between the inside and outside sections of the kennel where the stolen Jack Russell had been staying."

Huerta glared at Addison, who looked as if he wished someone in a black Suburban would kidnap *him*.

"I guess I should have checked the kennel more closely," he mumbled.

"Miss ... er ..." The female officer standing behind Huerta was around my age. Her pressed suit combined with her cop's poker face told me she was probably a detective.

"Doctor," I corrected. "Dr. Kulkarni."

"Dr. Kulkarni, have you ever heard of C.A.L.F.?"

"Like a baby cow?"

"The Companion Animal Liberation Front. They believe that pet ownership is animal abuse. This little cow is their calling card."

"Never heard of them," I said.

"They're new, out of Portland. They've been kidnapping pets and releasing them outside of city limits."

My blood started to simmer. "Because becoming coyote food is so much better than being a pet?"

The detective said, "We've been following reports of their activity as it moves south. We've been wondering how long it would take for the movement to turn up in L.A."

"I've been reporting pet snatchings for a month," I said.

Huerta cleared her throat. "We weren't certain there was a connection before now."

"And the theft of plain old mutts, redeemed from the shelter for a twenty, doesn't meet the thousand-dollar threshold for criminal action." I was fairly shaking by that point.

"Wasn't that a voter initiative?" the detective asked.

"The masses are asses. Look," I said. "There's a black Suburban with a stolen Irish Setter heading north into the Hollywood Hills, as we speak ..." I fell silent as another piece of the puzzle fell into place. "Fryman Canyon Park," I said.

"Excuse me?" Huerta said.

"Last week, one of my patients said his dog had disappeared from the back yard. The dog had jumped the fence before, so we figured it had escaped. But this morning he called to say that a hiker had found the dog wandering around Fryman Canyon Park."

"That's a long way from West Hollywood," Huerta said.

"Exactly. There's no way the dog wandered all that way itself."

Huerta and the detective exchanged a look.

"So," I continued. "C.A.L.F. has Jennifer Howard's dog and probably Pythagoras, too, and they're releasing pets in Fryman Canyon Park. What are we going to do about it?"

Huerta looked me in the eye. "*You* are going to go back to your practice and stay out of this. Maybe send an email to your patients warning them against leaving their dogs unattended. *We* will deal with this matter."

"But the Suburban was headed up Laurel Canyon. They're probably dumping dogs as we speak."

"We'll handle it," Huerta said. "But this isn't a job for a civilian."

The detective crossed her arms over her chest. Her expression told me she wouldn't be any help in the matter. Giving Huerta one last glare, I rose and left before I said something we all would regret.

Outside the police station, a hot pink Boxster splayed diagonally across two parking spaces. I was about to lob a snide remark at the two women standing beside it when I recognized them both.

"Dr. K!" Ms. Howard called, waving.

"They released you?" I'd left a message for my lawyer friend, but hadn't heard back from her.

"Dr. Finney decided not to press charges."

I turned to the willowy blonde in the silk suit that matched her Porsche. "Doctor?"

The blonde smiled self consciously. "I have PhDs in psychology and animal psychology. Deputy Huerta asked me to come in to give a statement. After explaining what had happened, I asked to speak to Jennifer. It was all a misunderstanding. Besides, we animal people have to stick together."

"Did you get Sinead?" Ms. Howard asked. She squinted toward the clinic van.

"Yeah, about that ..." I glanced back through the glass doors of the station, which did not appear to be bustling with deputies rousing themselves for a dog rescue. "Come with me, both of you. I'll explain what happened on the way."

"Where are we going?" Dr. Finney asked as we piled into the van.

"Fryman Canyon Park." I glanced at Ms. Howard in the rear-view mirror. She looked worried, and I didn't blame her. The pink drained from her cheeks as I explained what happened.

"It wasn't that long ago," I said. "If they released her there, chances are she won't have gone far."

One hoped. On the other hand, a lot could happen to a loose pet in a wilderness area. We sped back past the place where I'd had the surreal encounter with the shepherdess, up into hills covered with sun-flattened yellow grass, and emerged among the trees. As we hung a left onto Mulholland, I used my hands-free set to call Tate.

"What's up, boss lady?" he asked.

"I'm headed up to Fryman Canyon Park to catch a dognapper," I said. "Call Deputy Huerta and tell her to meet us there."

"She's not going to like that."

"Probably not," I agreed. "But I go the extra mile for my patients."

The Fryman Canyon Park parking lot came up fast. We slowed as we approached the gate. The late afternoon sun was low in the sky and painting everything with a warm orange glow. The parking lot was deserted, except for …

"That's the Suburban that was following me," Jennifer Howard said.

Dr. Finney said, "I've seen it before, as well."

I pulled up to a clump of trees at the side of the road. A dog was barking in the distance. An Irish Setter? Or a Jack Russell? I eased out of the van, motioning for the other two to follow. We peeked through the trees.

The back door of the Suburban was open, and someone was standing behind it. The van was shaking, and as we drew closer, I could make out two voices: those of a young man and a mightily annoyed Jack Russell.

"That's Pythagoras!" Dr. Finney whispered.

"Wait here," I said.

I put my shoulders back, pulled myself up to my full five-foot two-inch height, and stepped out from behind the trees.

"Excuse me," I called in my most authoritative Doctor voice.

The van stopped shaking. The man peered out from behind the door. He was a pasty-faced kid, probably in his early twenties, with a mess of tangled hair and a complicated beard. He recognized me.

"Where are Sinead and Pythagoras?" I demanded.

"Who?"

"The Irish Setter and the Jack Russell you stole."

"I didn't steal anything. I liberated two sovereign beings. Of course I wouldn't expect a lackey of the veterinary industrial complex to—AAAGH! Get off me! Get off me, you little—"

"Pythagoras!" Dr. Finney cried. "Let my dog go!"

It was Pythagoras who actually had the upper hand, or rather the upper part of the dognapper's hand, and she didn't seem inclined to release it. Jack Russells don't lock their jaws like pit bulls do, but they're tenacious as hell, and their bite can do real damage. I ran.

"Hold still," I told the young man. "Panicking makes it worse." I squeezed between him and the door, and took Pythagoras under one arm

"That's easy for you to say! The little monster should be put down!"

Under normal circumstances, I might have agreed, but in this case I was willing to give the dog the benefit of the doubt.

"What's your name?" I asked over the buzzsaw sound of Jack Russell growling.

He sniffed. "Brandon."

"Brandon, I'm going to turn this dog onto its back, slowly, which should cause it to let go of your hand. Turn your arm along with me, all right?"

His lip trembled, but he nodded. Slowly I turned Pythagoras onto her back. The dog let go, and I closed my hand around her mouth.

"Miss Howard," I called. "There's a muzzle and a medical kit in the back of the van. Please bring them here. Dr. Finney, please come and get your dog."

Once Pythagoras was muzzled and leashed, I cleaned Brandon's wounds and applied antibiotic cream and a bandage.

"That thing better have it shots," Brandon grumbled.

I looked a question at Dr. Finney, who nodded. I said, "Animal Control will have to investigate the bite, but I'm pretty sure they'll agree that these were extenuating circumstances. I'll be happy to speak to them, if you like."

"Thank you," Dr. Finney said.

"But that thing mauled me!" Brandon cried.

I said, "You'll live. Not sure about your upholstery though." Inside the Suburban, Pythagoras had done her worst—gouged holes in the leather, pulled out and shredded the stuffing, and ripped open a baggie of multicolored zip ties. "Oh!" I cried as a foul odor assailed me.

"Did someone have a little tummy trouble?" Dr. Finney asked, holding Pythagoras clear of her immaculate pink suit.

I said, "*Someone* has been snatching dogs with a nasty stomach bug. Pythagoras probably picked it up while riding around in the kidnap mobile. When this is all over, drop by the clinic, and we'll get her sorted." I looked at Brandon. "Wish I could say the same for the other pets you've been dumping in these woods."

"They're free, now," Brandon said.

"They're someone's dinner," I retorted. "And even if they've escaped the coyotes and mountain lions, most pets wouldn't have the first idea how to feed themselves in the wild."

"Spoken like a true lackey of the—ow!"

"Sorry," I said. "Had to make sure that bandage was tight enough."

A volley of happy barking erupted from a clump of trees. A thrilled-to-be-alive Irish Setter bounded toward us, looking none the worse for wear.

"Sinead!" Ms. Howard cried. I watched as dog and owner came together for an ecstatic reunion. If there had been any doubt in my mind that the Irish Setter really did belong to Ms. Howard, it dissolved.

Just then, tires crunched over the dirt and gravel parking lot. Deputy Huerta pulled the black and white to a stop and exited the driver's seat, Addison following close behind.

"This is Brandon," I said as she opened her mouth, no doubt to dress me down. "He's admitted to stealing and illegally dumping multiple animals in this park. Also, a medic should take a look at his hand."

"So Pythagoras doesn't really do long division?" Tate asked that evening over veggie burgers and beer. He sounded genuinely crestfallen, and I felt a bit sorry for him.

"Yes and no," Dr. Finney said. "At first I thought I had a doggy genius on my hands. But being a scientist, and an animal behaviorist in specific, I knew I had to put my theory to the test. The truth is, Pythagoras is quite clever, and like many animals, she has a sense of numerosity, that is, the idea of quantities of things. But no dog has yet shown the ability to understand and manipulate numerical symbols."

"Oh," Tate said.

"But she does have another gift." Dr. Finney snatched a fry from Tate's plate and dunked it into his ketchup. "She is uncommonly adept at reading my mind."

"Whoa," Tate said.

I raised a skeptical eyebrow.

She said, "Dogs are incredibly perceptive and can read people better than we can read ourselves. Did you know that dogs have evolved the ability to use the tufts of hairs above their eyes to express emotion like we do with eyebrows?"

"Whoa," Tate said again.

"So how does she solve the equations?" I asked.

"I'm still trying to crack the exact code, but she's reading something in my expression or voice that tells her the answer that I'm looking for. Her gift is reading her human. I know it's a bit of a cheat to call her a counting dog, but the gimmick gets people to pay attention while I talk about animal behavior and care."

"That's cool," Tate said. Only then did I notice how closely they were sitting on the bench on the other side of the table.

"I'm sorry I thought you were abusing her," Jennifer Howard said.

"I wish you hadn't stolen my dog, but I'm glad you're ready to take action when you think an animal is being mistreated." She stopped to snitch another fry. "I'm using some of the advertising money my videos have made on Dog Tok to start a pet advocacy organization. We want to educate people about animals' emotional and intellectual needs. I'd be honored if you helped."

"Sure!" Jennifer said.

"Can I help too?" Tate asked.

"Fancy being our media manager?" His grin said that he fancied it very much. "And Dr. Kulkarni, I'd love it if you could lend us your expertise, as well."

"I'll drink to that," I said.

We all raised our glasses.

TRUE GARBAGE

Stanton McCaffery

Richard opened the manilla envelope. Before he could look inside, the dog barked at a passerby. "Henry, you have to stop that," he said through an open window. The envelope was in a waste-high pile of garbage. Inside, it wasn't what he was looking for. It was a warranty for a fridge, not correspondence from his mother. He dropped it back into the pile of trash and brought his dead father's dog inside his dead father's house.

The man had passed two weeks prior, but he'd only known for a week. The mailman called it in, said mail was piling up and that the dog inside wouldn't stop howling. Coroner said he had a stroke and laid on the floor for a week, was lucky the dog hadn't started to eat him.

In another pile of trash, Richard found paper with handwriting. It was an assignment of his from grade school—fiction he portrayed as fact. A story about his dog. A dog he didn't have—not at the time.

It was the first story he constructed to conceal his ugly life, from others and from himself.

"I inherited him," Richard said to people at the dog park. He turned away from them, trying to hide the red patches on his face—eczema that flared up when he was stressed. He was trying as much as possible to avoid anyone looking at him. But there's no avoiding stares with a dog like Henry, an over-sized Italian Pointer that loved to dig and bellow in the faces of other dogs.

"Maybe he's anxious," a woman said, from behind him.

Richard turned around. She had a beagle standing at her feet. He wished people kept their thoughts to themselves. It only made matters worse, pointing out the obvious.

"They're all a lot of work," the woman said, "but it's worth it, you'll see."

He didn't believe her. People lie to make you feel better. To make themselves feel better.

"I'm Stacy," the woman said.

Richard said his name and bent to pet the Beagle. When the dog released a high-pitched bark, he stood.

"Rose, what's the matter?" Stacy said. "I'm sorry, usually she's so friendly with people."

"Must be something about me," Richard said.

"How often are you here?" she asked.

Richard itched his forehead and looked at Henry. "Oh, I don't really know. I guess like once a week."

"Okay, well, when you figure that out, I'm here almost every evening. I guess I'll see you around."

Richard stood by Henry in the empty dog park in the rain, looking at the parking lot. His toes were getting wet through his sneakers. The woman said she was there every day. Maybe she regretted telling him that? Maybe she could see through him to his broken insides and wanted to avoid having to look again?

He glanced at his phone. A notification of a new email. "You are a fraud," said the message. "I want my money back." He moved the email to spam and pocketed his phone. He thought of when he was younger and saw his father so angry he could kill someone. He could feel himself turning into the same person. As long as he kept his story up, he believed, he could keep that person from coming out. He could keep reality hidden.

He rolled up his jacket sleeve, itched the eczema on his arm, and rolled it back down. As he was leashing Henry, Stacey pulled into the lot. "I thought I'd be the only one here," she said.

"Well, he needs to get out, right?"

She told him she liked that he put the dog's needs first. "People think they look silly standing out here in the rain. It's nice there are other people that don't care about looking silly."

They made small talk. He told her he was an executive coach and motivational speaker. "That must mean you've really got your shit together," she said.

She told him she was a hospice nurse. "Well," he said, "that must mean you're really kind."

She laughed. "Maybe. What it really means is that I've toughened up from watching so many people die."

The morning they were to meet at a lake to walk the dogs, Richard checked his Google reviews. Someone said he didn't know what he was talking about. They said he made everything up.

It left him frustrated and puzzled, knots in his brain and gut. Didn't everyone make things up? People embellished their resumes. People exaggerated. They talked themselves up to get hired or promoted. Why did it always seem like he was the only one that never got away with it? He wanted to be something better, something more than his father, but it would never happen with people always ruining everything for him.

It made him want to cancel, tell Stacey he was sick. But that went against a core tenant included in his talks: do something even if you don't feel like it.

They walked the lake. The dogs waded in to their hips. Henry walked through mud and sniffed high blades of grass, Rose following suit while yelping at squirrels.

When they started away from the lake, Henry stayed near the water. He whined, tried to move, and made a high-pitched bark.

Richard walked into the mud and looked at the dog's legs. "Some asshole's fishing wire," he said.

Stacey walked over and took a folded knife from her pocket, flicked it open and cut the line. "Always have it on me," she said. "Helps get dogs out of whatever messes they get into."

Richard asked her to go for drinks. "Something without the dogs," he said with a laugh. "Somewhere we can get to know each other."

When they went to the bar, they sat, talked. Richard gave a variation on his standard mythology. He came from a strong family. His father was an officer in the marines and a detective. When he retired, he was a consultant to police departments. "The man was the core inspiration behind what I do today."

Giving her the mythology—giving anyone the mythology—made him feel like a real person. Like he could stand up straight. Like his skin wasn't red and rashy.

Then he told her he was writing a book about his father. He was going to self-publish it. That much was true. Richard hoped it would take his career up a notch, give him something to sell when he made his speeches.

A man near them sat with his head back. He opened his eyes into slits when Richard finished. "Hey, I know you. Yeah, you're Richard Deptford. Hey man, I thought your dad stayed at home and collected disability."

"I'm sorry, you must have me confused with someone else."

"Nah man, no way. I remember you. You don't remember me? I can't believe you don't remember me."

Richard took his coat. The man continued to talk as he stood and put his hand on Stacey's shoulder, said he thought they should go. "Buddy, I think you're confused. You've mistaken me for somebody else."

The man shook his alcohol-reddened face. He reached his hand, took Stacey by the wrist and said, "I'd say *you're* mistaken sweetheart, being with somebody doesn't know who they are."

Richard stuck his chest out. He stepped to the man in two strides. Stacey's eyes grew when Richard grabbed the man by the front of his shirt and lifted him from his seat.

"I said, you shut your mouth, you hear me? I told you to stop talking. You're drunk and you don't know what you're saying."

He pushed the man into the seat and let go of his shirt. Stacey tugged his arm. He stepped back, towards her. He pointed at the man. "I see you again and ..."

Stacey began walking towards the exit, pulling Richard behind her like luggage at an airport terminal.

As they walked out, the man said from behind, "Should have remembered that temper." Then he belched and laughed.

Stacey paused in the parking lot. Richard had already gotten in the truck and pressed the button for the keyless ignition. He could feel her eyes pressing on him through the window. He kept his straight ahead.

He could hear every single move she made as she pulled the door handle, opened the door, sat down, and put on her seat belt. She breathed in and out. He watched from the corner of his eyes as her chest rose and fell, like calm waves in an ocean expected to swell before long.

Minutes into the drive, she spoke. "People can hide things because they're things that hurt them. Maybe they hide things because they're working hard to be something else. Believe me, I understand that."

He brought her home and expected it to be the last time he'd see her. Any calls would go unanswered. He put the truck in park in front of her place.

His anger was quiet and no longer towards the drunk. This was a sour anger that would fester and poison. He was angry at himself and the life he was born into. He could feel the eczema on his arms and face flame as he sat.

Instead of opening the door, she turned, she opened her mouth to speak and paused, like she was putting her words in the right order. She started again. "I like you Rich. Whatever you're hiding, you don't have to hide."

He kept one hand on the steering wheel. "I'm not hiding anything."

She pulled her lips in. "I put a baby up for adoption," she said. "He's grown now, after somebody else took care of him."

Richard turned to face her. The sour anger inside him was mute. He placed a hand on hers. "You didn't have to tell me that."

"No," she said, "I didn't. But I wanted you to know something true about me."

He told her his mother left him and his father, that his childhood was a sad mess. He told her his father was a hoarder and that he'd inherited his mounds of garbage. He didn't tell her that he suspected his father wasn't telling the whole truth. Nor did he tell her he built his career on lies and that all of it was slowly but surely coming undone. And that that undoing had him terrified.

"See," she said. "It's not like you killed someone."

"I'm spending a lot of time at the house now. I'm throwing things out, but mostly I'm trying to find something that will give me an idea of where my mother is ... or was."

She looked pleased. She opened the door and stood. "Let me know if you'd like help."

They worked their way to the basement where they found piles of clothes in between metal filing cabinets that stood among the rubbish like headstones in a forgotten cemetery. Some of the clothes were his. Some he'd never seen before. Richard put them all in garbage bags and brought them to the dumpster.

He thought about his book that he was about to publish. Nothing about it was true. At some point he would have to face everything he made up about himself and his family, but the time hadn't come yet. He wasn't ready for all of the truth. Even if he knew it was there.

When he came back to the basement, Stacey was going through the filing cabinets. She held a metal tool with a wooden handle. "Wonder why he put this there," she said.

It was a tool for filing down wood, a chisel—nine inches long and pointed at the end. It looked sturdy. "He'd pick up odd hobbies when I was little, then never go anywhere with them."

He took it from her. There was rust on the metal. It came off on his fingers in a reddish-brown powder. Was it rust?

A voice inside whispered to Richard. It said he knew why the wood file was there.

He knew what his father was, what he had done, but Richard chose to ignore it, to deny the voice existed like he denied every painful part of his existence.

When they parted ways later, Richard checked his voicemail.

"Hello Richard, this is Ronald Vanderson, the Dean for New Students at Round Valley Community College. You had been booked for our fall orientation lecture series. I'm afraid we are going to have to remove you from the event. We had a former student call with some serious fraud allegations and we weren't able to verify a number of items on your resume."

Richard pressed stop. Then pressed the trash icon.

He breathed quickly. He told himself once he got the book out he would have more to say and that would make everything okay. They'd be things that people would believe. No one would listen to the fraud claims because how could they deny what he'd written. How could they deny his story?

Cleaning more with Stacey, rain emptied from clouds above the house. As if they held megatons of pressure for a lifetime and finally realized they weren't up to the job.

It was all nearly cleaned. Only papers remained. That and memories.

The dogs were outside in the rain and the mud. They tackled each other and ran and sniffed like they had known each other their entire lives. Like they could be themselves with each other.

Inside, Stacey and Richard assessed one final pile. One last summit to conquer. Richard took papers by the fistful and trashed them. Stacey looked at each piece with the scrutiny of an auditor.

He'd been nervous and ashamed at first, letting this near-stranger inside his father's home, allowing her to pour through the items of his childhood. But now he felt like there was nothing to be afraid of. Not with her. Whatever she found they would deal with, together.

"Is this yours, Richard?" she said. It was the paper he had found when he first started cleaning the house by himself, his second-grade essay about the dog he didn't have. "You didn't tell me you had a dog named Henry when you were a kid."

"I didn't. I mean, I didn't have one. I made it up."

"But your father named his dog Henry decades later. Richard, I think that's really special."

He couldn't deny that it was. His guard went down. He felt the muscles in his abdomen relax for what felt like the first time. For years, something in the back of his head was trying to figure out a way he could be himself. It was like he was trying to catch a rabbit. It always escaped him. He'd had neither the tools nor the skills to grab onto it. Now, the rabbit was in his grasp.

"It was like I needed to create this separate self," he said. "I was so ashamed. I wanted a life I could be proud of."

Then Henry howled from the yard. He was barking and running after Rose, but frantically. They weren't playing. They'd dug a massive hole in the yard. Rose had something in her mouth, something white. Something broke inside Richard like an icepick struck a live wire.

He and Stacey went to investigate. She ran after Rose. He went to the hole.

He knew what was in the hole before he got to it. He knew all along, somewhere inside, somewhere deep inside his brain. Like when you know you're going to have a bad day. Or when you can feel a storm coming in your bones.

He'd denied it. Like he denied everything. Denied who his father was. Denied who he was.

His abdominal muscles went tight. In his mind, the rabbit had gotten loose again as he stood over the skeleton wearing his mother's clothes—jeans and a sweatshirt. He put his hand on his mouth and cursed. He wanted to rush Stacey inside and tell her there was nothing in the hole, but it was too late. She went to it.

"Jesus fucking Christ, Richard, these are human remains. Look! Look at this! There's a hole in the skull."

It was the width of an index finger.

She didn't have to say it. He knew. *The wood file.*

The rain pelted Richard as he went somewhere in his past. He was in his bed, listening to his parents argue. Then, later the same night, he heard a shovel against dirt.

Richard let the rain and the truth beat on him. His mother never left. She'd been there all along. But that wasn't the myth he lived by. It would all come out. The shame of it. He built the structure of his life on bricks of disintegrating sand. He'd never sell a book about his father the hero. Because his father wasn't a hero. He was a killer.

"We need to go inside and we need to call the police!"

"I don't want to do that," he said, while still looking down at his dead mother. "I think ... we should bury it again."

"You can't do that," she said. "I know it's hard, but it's not right to pretend it's not here. This isn't normal, Richard. I know you don't want to face that, but you have to."

She went to touch his shoulder, but he pulled away. She tried to touch his face and he slapped her hand.

"You don't understand," he said, crying. "I can't let people know about this. I can't. No one. People will think I'm a freak. People will *know* I'm a freak."

She came to him again and tried to hug him, but he took her by the shoulders, and he shook her. She could have been the one. He was ready to open up to her, but this, this was a bridge too far.

Then he put his hands around her neck. He didn't want to do it, but he did it anyway. He squeezed and he shook. They struggled and they fell into the muddy hole.

Stacey slapped and she gasped. She looked stunned, betrayed.

Rose leapt into the hole and sunk her teeth into Richard's leg. He turned and swiped at her, giving Stacey enough time to reach into her pocket. She took out the knife she used to cut the fishing wire, fidgeted with it to get it open. When Richard put his hands back around her neck she drove it into his carotid artery.

She rolled out from under him as blood shot from his neck to mix with the rain and the mud. She called the police. She took off her jacket and went back into the hole. He was still alive and she tried to keep him that way. She took her jacket and held it to the knife wound.

"It didn't have to be like this," she said.

But Richard knew that wasn't true. It had to end like this because of how it started. It's what he inherited.

"I didn't know what else to do," he said, as he passed into darkness.

THE FIRST APARTMENT

Sherry Roberts

We began our life together feasting on grilled cheese sandwiches in a cold and lonely Minnesota bus depot. I loved my new husband, Lars Larson, but I truly missed the luxurious warmth of my grandmother's Thanksgiving table: the glow of candles, the delicious aroma of the turkey, the camaraderie of my legion of cousins who couldn't pass the yams without a generous portion of outlandish storytelling.

Shivering in a paper-thin coat that had been quite adequate back home in Georgia, I watched more snow than I ever dreamed existed pile up on the streets outside. "What if it doesn't stop?" I worried.

Lars, the idiot who lured me here, just laughed. "Eat up. We should get back to the Ho Hum before the roads get bad."

You might have already guessed: the Ho Hum Hotel was not the Ritz.

And so began my life in a foreign land, also called Last Chance, Minnesota.

The next day we set out with two missions: buy a warm winter coat to replace my Southern jacket and procure our first apartment. It was Friday, and our furniture was scheduled to arrive on Monday. That's when we discovered Last Chance had a housing shortage.

Wearing a new down parka and lug-soled lumberjack boots, I toured one of our few housing options: a drab two-bedroom duplex apartment that looked like a palace compared to the others we'd seen. The landlady assured us that the neighbor next door, a quiet woman of considerable age named Birdie, would be no trouble. "She sleeps most of the time," said Leda the landlady.

Lars could see my disappointment as we walked through the small kitchen, an uninspiring living room, and down a hall to two tiny bedrooms and a bath. "We really can't be choosey, Sam," he whispered. "We'll look for something better in a few months."

The apartment did not give me the cozy feeling that I had hoped for in our first home. I sighed. Lars took that as a yes, and I tried to think positively. As Grandma

G used to say, *When the good Lord gives you lemons, pitch them in the neighbor's yard to rot and head to the nearest bar.*

The snow did stop by Monday. Lars dropped me off at the duplex with a kiss and a smile. He was geared up to be the best assistant principal the Last Chance Elementary School had ever seen. While he was herding small humans, I would be in charge of directing the burly ones: the movers.

As I approached the duplex, I found the front door wide open. Power cords slithered out of the apartment through the snow to a loud generator in the front yard. Climbing over the snow bank, wading through the unshoveled sidewalk, and stepping over the cords, I shouted, "Hello?"

"C'mon in," yelled Leda. Our landlady was crawling on the living room floor with a man she introduced as Fergus. They were in the process of unrolling, tugging, laying, and tacking down a carpet.

"It's freezing in here," I said, hunkering deeper into my coat.

Without pausing in her work, Leda said, "Had to shut off the power to fix the furnace. Ferg and I need electricity for our tools. Luckily, Ferg has a generator."

"What are you doing?" I asked, pointing to the carpet. "This wasn't here when we viewed the apartment on Friday."

"Nope. This is a special surprise for you two newlyweds." It was an ugly drab-colored carpet.

Suddenly Fergus swore. "Got another rip here, Leda, but I can patch it. The couch will hide it." He gave the carpet a jerk that made me wince. "I told you buying this used carpet from the dentist's office was risky. This stuff has already been stretched to hell and back."

"Oh hush, Ferg. This will look real nice when we're done." Looking up at me, Leda said, "You did bring a couch, didn't you?"

I headed outside, plunged up to my knees in a snow drift, and dialed Lars on my cell phone. He answered after the third ring, "How's the place look? Has the furniture arrived?"

"We've got a problem. We don't have any power or heat, it's twenty-five degrees, and we have a carpet in the living room."

I could hear kids charging down the hall in the background. "I don't remember a carpet. What color?"

"Dental beige."

Ordering the children to "walk, not run," Lars the ever positive one said to me, "We'll figure it out. Just make sure the movers set up the bedroom and find the extra blankets. I'll bring pizza home for dinner. We'll have it in bed."

We ended the call with our usual sign-off. He said in a sexy growl, "You didn't know what you were getting into when you married me." And I replied, "No, *you* didn't know what you were getting into."

I knocked the snow off my boots before entering the apartment again and met a stranger coming down the hall. He nodded hello to me then reported to Leda, "Don't have enough of that Misty Blue paint to finish the bathroom. But I might have some leftover Cosmic Cerulean back at the house."

"That'll work, Cecil," said Leda. "Whatever you got. Put it on one wall as an accent."

Cecil left, and I walked through the living room and down the short hall toward the bathroom. "You're painting the bathroom?"

"Just freshening it up," Leda said.

I poked my head into the ugliest bathroom I'd ever seen. "Um, is Cecil coming back?" I called.

"Tomorrow probably."

On the floor of the bathroom Cecil had left paint stirrers stuck to newspapers, open paint cans, and uncleaned paint brushes already growing stiff.

I was about to tell Leda that we didn't agree to all these renovations but was interrupted by the arrival of the movers. Without a word, they trekked through the open kitchen door, stepped over Leda and Fergus, and followed me to the spare bedroom. There was nowhere else to put our moving boxes and living room furniture. By the time the movers finished, our belongings were piled to the ceiling.

One young but exceptionally fit mover stopped in the hallway and asked, "What's that for? Kinda narrow for a closet."

"Where?"

He nodded toward a gap at the end of the hall that I hadn't noticed before. It ran from ceiling to floor, about a foot wide. I couldn't imagine what that dark space was for and didn't dare step through it to explore.

I knew there had been a wall there when we originally looked at the apartment, so what happened to it? "Leda," I called, "where's the rest of our apartment?"

Swatting at her dusty jeans and pushing her rolled flannel shirtsleeves above her bony elbows, Leda walked up beside me. "That's my place."

"We're neighbors?"

Shoving her chin-length, gray-streaked, frizzy hair behind her ears, she explained, "I live in California. Just spend a few months in Minnesota to manage my properties.

So I took a little space off the back of both duplexes and built my own studio. Gonna save me a ton of money." She pulled a flashlight from her back pocket and cast light through the dark gap revealing a large, dim room. It contained a space heater, sleeping bag, camp stove, miniature refrigerator, folding table, and toilet and sink in the corner.

"You're camping back there?"

"It's cozy, all right," she said with a note of pride in her voice.

"But ..."

"Don't worry. I got my own entrance, and I'll wall up this space when we're done with renovations. I'll build you some cute little bookshelves here."

I was a culinary blogger and recorded podcasts on baking and cooking. None of my cookbooks had a hope of fitting in that slim space.

Eventually, the movers left. Fergus wished me luck, gathered his cords and tools, and closed the front door. Cecil never came back. I hadn't seen the furnace repairman all day and hoped Leda wasn't doing the job herself. Leda assured me we would have heat tomorrow, then she stepped through the gap to her apartment and slid a sheet of plywood across the space. Finally, I was alone, and I wanted to cry.

Later, bundled in bed with Lars and a large pepperoni pizza, I wondered what Grandma G would have thought of my first home. An advocate for privacy and warmth, she probably would have said, *Samantha Sue Bailey, pack your bags and get your butt back to the Ho Hum.*

It was tempting. The temperature that night was to drop into the teens.

In the weeks between Thanksgiving and Christmas, Lars settled into his new job. I spent my days shutting out the cacophony of the workers, unboxing the kitchen, and planning podcasts. But I couldn't record. All the renovations took longer—and were louder—than Leda predicted, mainly because she skimped on materials, hired unreliable help, and bought used appliances. I began to worry about missing deadlines.

Fergus helped me position the couch over the unsightly carpet patch. Cecil finally returned a week later and did his worst on the bathroom. I only stepped in the open paint can once, one night in the dark, and had learned to automatically shut my eyes when I showered to avoid the ocular clash of orange tiles and Cosmic Cerulean walls.

I baked, testing cookie recipes for my Christmas blog and podcast. Leda popped in through the Mouth of Hell, as Lars now called the gap, at various times of the day, often following the aroma of baking. She never passed the kitchen without snatching, uninvited, a handful of cookies cooling on the table. Twice she dropped in for dinner, again uninvited, and took the leftovers home with her.

Leda didn't seem concerned about the invasion of mice I heard and saw, but she was adamant that I not use peanuts in my baking. Apparently, she was allergic to peanuts, not mice. I immediately went out and bought mouse poison and a pound of peanuts.

At night, Lars regaled me with stories of adorable schoolchildren and potential juvenile delinquents, the latter group striking a kinship in me. Although the furnace had finally started producing heat again, I still wore layers to bed. Lars, a native Minnesotan who ran around in shorts on ten-degree days, teased me about my "thin Southern blood."

One night I woke to find someone leaning over me. It was Leda wearing one of my flannel nightgowns.

"Leda?" I said groggily.

"Mind if I use your bathroom?" she whispered. "Mine is clogged up."

The next morning Lars didn't believe me when I reported our nighttime visitor.

"That's it," I fumed. "I can't take anymore. You get to go off and spend all day with little brats and I'm stuck with Leda."

He treated me as if I were a pack of rioting third graders. "Now, Sam, calm down. Let's be good neighbors."

I didn't tell Lars how Grandma G used to punish Grandpa when he acted unreasonable—how she would put hot sauce in his soup or lace his garlic mashed potatoes with laxative. As Grandma G used to say, *Food is my weapon.*

When Leda gave no indication she was leaving and had yet to close the hole between our apartments, I invited her to lunch and began planning recipes. Should I put mouse poison in the Snickerdoodles or bake peanuts in the hot dish? In Minnesota, a hot dish is a casserole.

After our lunch, which I'd served with the elegance of a high tea, Leda said she felt tired and went back to her studio for a nap. She was in her sixties, and an afternoon snooze was not out of order. I didn't hear any more from her for the rest of the day. Or the next day. I was curious, but I also was a big believer in plausible deniability. So, although I pressed my ear to the plywood, I stayed on my side of the gap. I took the peanuts and mouse poison to the landfill.

After a quiet week I boarded up the gap, nailed it shut, and painted the wall a lovely sage green. In fact, I liked the green so much I carried it over into the bathroom. When Lars came home and saw my decorating changes, he asked, "Did you get Leda's approval for this?"

I shrugged innocently. "I think she went back to California."

That night Lars raved about the chicken cordon bleu and the Death by Chocolate cake. I just smiled. I did get my cooking skills from my grandmother.

TO THE CASTLE BORNE

J.R. Parsons

"Yo ho, yo ho, an EveryEats life for me," Angie sang as she drove across the bridge to Bellville Island Thursday evening.

She patted the Pirate Mike's Seafood box on the passenger seat. She didn't understand why anyone would pay twice the cost of a meal for a five-mile delivery, but she wasn't complaining. Since being laid off from her job at the Newtown Beach Yacht Club amid the latest economic downturn, this gig was the only thing that put bucks in the bank.

And singing kept her sane. Especially singing made-up ditties on delivery runs. Earlier that evening, she had worked a Chick-Chick delivery into a verse from Shania Twain's "I Feel Like a Woman."

Minutes later Angie's phone beeped, signaling her imminent arrival at the delivery destination. Seeing approaching headlights, she eased over to give the oncoming van room to pass on the narrow street. Instead of waving thanks, the driver shouted something unintelligible and hit the gas, his broad face peevish under a red Mia Ristorante cap.

Angie sighed. Some people shed misery like Itzi, her Corgi, shed hair. Shrugging, she drove the short way to where Mariners Drive ended, made a U-turn, and parked. Exiting her vehicle, she did a double-take. Somebody needed to give England back its castle.

As she negotiated the iron gate to access the grounds, she checked the delivery instructions for warnings about moats or drawbridges. (Seriously, it paid to double-check those things. When money's no object, obstacles can get crazy.) All she saw was a message about dropping the food off on the porch. And a $20 tip. *Woohoo.*

Humming ABBA's "Dancing Queen," she bounced up a lilac hedged castle walkway, illuminated by sculpted lanterns. And found the castle's entryway wide open. Inside, lights blazed.

"EveryEats!" Angie called out.

When no one appeared, she set the box down, shouted, "Food's on the porch," and stepped off the landing. Behind her she heard a gasp, followed by thumping and scraping.

Turning back, Angie shouted, "Hello. Is someone hurt in there?"

A woman's voice came from somewhere inside the home: "Oh, thank God. Please get help. Hurry." She sounded scared.

Hands shaking, Angie called 911.

Forty minutes later she was still at the castle house, answering questions posed by a Newtown Beach police detective.

"Do you often make deliveries to the island, Ms. Peretti?" Detective Grayson asked. Dressed in light gray slacks and a green plaid bomber jacket, he loomed over her by a good foot or more. His manner suggested that he had assessed her ripped jeans, t-shirt, and ball cap and found them suspicious.

"First and last time, Detective," Angie assured him. "I'd make more money not crossing the bridge. Every minute I'm stuck here is costing me."

"Yes, well, I'm afraid it can't be helped. The Armsteads are—"

"Rich, powerful, important?"

Grayson's mouth turned down. "I was going to say distraught, Ms. Peretti. The wife, especially, is inconsolable."

"Yeah. Must be tough having your castle breached," Angie said.

That earned her a sharp look from Grayson. "How did you know the robbers broke in?" he demanded.

Angie rolled her eyes. "It's just an expression. Look at this place. It's a baby Buckingham Palace."

Grayson's lips twitched in what might have been a smile. Angie gave it a 50-50 chance. The detective cleared his throat. "Yes, well, let's move on shall we, Ms. Peretti. You told the responding officers that you got here about seven-thirty?"

"Seven thirty-five," said Angie, scrolling on her phone. "Nope, sorry, the delivery app says seven thirty-seven." She flashed Grayson a rueful smile. "And it's only wrong when it comes to calculating drivers' wages."

"All right. So, when you arrived at seven thirty-seven, did you see anything suspicious? Anyone hanging around? Or running away?"

Angie shifted weight from one leg to the other. Her feet were killing her. "Sorry, I didn't see anything. And before you ask, I didn't hear anything either. Not until Mrs. Armstead called for help."

"And the front door was wide open when you arrived?"

Angie nodded, remembering how the entryway shone like a bright moon within the dark surroundings.

Grayson finished jotting notes and looked up. "Okay, that's all for now. But hang around. I may have more questions after I interview the victims."

Angie glanced around the towering foyer. Aside from a brass and marble console table, a solitary, stiff-backed mid-century chair, and spills of crushed cut flowers scattered on the gray tiles, the entryway was bare. And chilly. Crime scene techs trekked in and out the open front door, clothed in a confusing perfume of acrid chemicals, sweet lilac, and ocean brine. "In here?" she asked.

Grayson frowned. "No. I don't want you in my team's way."

Motioning for her to follow him, he slid open a double pocket door off the entryway and led her into a paneled study. Three individuals waited, dwarfed by a forest of oversized mahogany furniture. The hapless trio was cut from the same cloth, Angie observed: toned, carelessly fashionable, and now seriously annoyed by the intrusion. Grayson guided her to a wing chair near a fireplace with fluted columns, told her to stay put, then crossed to where the Armsteads huddled on a cognac leather sofa. Angie's discomfort increased when her gaze settled on the fireplace. She stared open-mouthed at the massive hearth; her Prius would fit inside the stone cavern.

She sat back in the chair, exhaled deeply, and tried to relax. Before long, she became aware of the low murmur of voices. Detective Grayson was conducting his interviews. Rising from the wing chair, she approached the custom-built bookcases flanking the fireplace. The shelves spanned an interminable wall, the one-inch planks spaced floor to ceiling, fairly sagging under the weight of classic literature and reference tomes in matched leather covers. Here and there, patches of modern books intruded, looking as out-of-place as Angie herself felt. One section caught her interest.

Angie stood and examined the orphaned book group. *Handling Storms at Sea*, *Heavy Weather Sailing*. *Storm Tactics*. The yacht club marina where she had worked kept a general library of nautical books. In contrast, Armstead's collection was small and specific. The titles brought a Great Big Sea song to her lips, a lament about a sailor's seasick wife trapped on a boat excursion around the bay and thinking she would die. With the song bobbing in her head, Angie sang under her breath as she traced the last two book titles with her fingers: *Sailing a Serious Ocean* and *Your Offshore Doctor*. Life and death stuff.

An experienced boat handler and dock attendant, Angie could not imagine what use the books had here given Southern California's calm waters. Of course, the same could be said for the expensive, leather-bound volumes entombed in the study. Judging by their immaculate condition, few had ever been opened—at least not in this century.

"It's no good badgering me," complained a penetrating voice. "I told you. I was upstairs when they broke in. Now kindly stop asking annoying questions and find the lowlife who invaded my home."

Startled, Angie reshelved the maritime medicine book and glanced around in time to catch Mrs. Armstead mid-tirade, lips twisted in a fierce snarl, eyes fiery. In the indirect light, she might have been mistaken for the castle dragon.

Grayson tried to explain that answering the questions would help him do just that. Before he'd finished speaking, a trim, older man seated beside the auburn-haired drago, leaned forward and said in a patronizing tone, "Really, Detective Grayson, this is too much. I must agree with my wife. We can tell you nothing else. Events happened so swiftly."

Grayson maintained his composure, though Angie figured he might later need antacids.

"Let's go through it one more time. Mr. Armstead," instructed the detective. "You said that when the robbers broke in you and Stephen were watching football ..." pausing, he consulted his notes "... in the game room at the back of the house. Is that accurate? Good. And you, Mrs. Armstead, you were upstairs getting ready for an evening out with your husband. And you didn't hear the break-in."

"Yes, as I told you several times," drawled Janice Armstead with apparent boredom.

Grayson turned back to Harold Armstead. "What time did the break-in occur, sir?"

Armstead worried his shirt cuff for a moment. "I believe it was around six. Yes, I'm sure of it. The Pats were up 14-10 with two minutes to go in the half. I heard a noise and went to investigate. That was when those thugs assaulted me and threatened to beat my head in if I didn't cooperate. They grabbed Stephen and bound us in the music room."

His wife jumped in. "I descended the stairs at six-fifteen. Two men accosted me on the bottom landing. They forced me to accompany them to where Harold and Stephen were being held. One of them was very rough with me."

"What happened after that?" Grayson asked.

Her husband snorted and glanced about the room. "Well, obviously they robbed the place. You can see for yourself. They took everything of value, everything they could carry. Paintings, of course. A Kooning, an early Kandinsky, a minor Rothko. They also took my Patek Philippe watches and my collection of rare jade figurines."

His wife mewled softly. "Not to mention my lovely jewelry, our priceless silver sets, and those darling Ming vases in the entryway. It's all gone."

"This is lame," interrupted the Armstead's teenage son. He sat slouched on the sofa, his thin form diminished even more by the oversized throw cushions. "And I'm starving."

Grayson stared at the teenager for a long moment. It was clear he was not impressed. "Yes, of course," he said. "The food you ordered was never eaten."

"We did not order food," argued Janice, accenting each word like a drumbeat. "Why would we? Harold and I were going out." She flapped a manicured hand and directed a dismissive look Angie's way. "That girl obviously delivered to the wrong address." Perhaps aware she sounded rude and ungrateful, she hurriedly added, "Not that we don't appreciate your coming to our aid. Thank goodness you found us. We could have been tied up forever."

"Or at least until your daily maid service showed up, dear," sniped Harold, ignorant of the daggers Janice directed his way.

Angie approached the group, conscious of the delivery box in her hand, and said quietly, "Well, somebody here ordered it."

Janice Armstead sniffed. "It wasn't me. I detest seafood. What about you, Harold. Did you order it?"

Her husband scoffed. "How could I? I was tied up the same as you, dear."

Mouth tightening, she swung around and glared at her son. "Stephen?"

"Me? No way," the teenager mumbled.

Detective Grayson's eyes found Angie's. "What about it, Ms. Peretti? Could you have delivered to the wrong address?"

Angie examined the sales receipt stapled to the sealed box. "Nope. The order was placed at 6:51 p.m. Delivery to this address."

"It has to be a mistake, Detective," Janice Armstead insisted. "No one here could have made that call. We were being held captive when Miss Peretti says the order was placed." She gave a small shudder. "Captives. In our own home."

Her son snickered. "Maybe the robbers got hungry, Mother, and ordered calamari. All you keep in the fridge is lousy diet food."

His father silenced him with a stern look, then appealed to Grayson in a plaintive voice. "I'm sure you can understand that we're on edge. This has been a shock. I know we've only lived here five years, but as they say, a man's home is his castle."

Armstead was standing now. Thrusting his hands wide, he turned in a slow half-circle, embracing the room. "I designed this study. Had it built special." His voice broke dramatically. "It's my sanctuary, a place to get away from everything." Sensing his wife's displeasure, he hastened to add, "For all of us. And now, now those bastards have ruined it."

Fighting the urge to roll her eyes, Angie dropped the Pirate Mike's box on the nearby captain's desk. A two-day-old copy of the *Newtown Times* lay open on the polished wood surface. The headline at the top of the local news section caught her attention: **Italian Restaurant Group in the Soup**. If that's about Pirate Jack's, she thought, I'll never get paid for this delivery.

Tuning out the ongoing drama, Angie skimmed the news story then wandered back to the fireplace. As she passed by a marble slab table, she realized that the thieves had been particular about what they made off with. Several ornate picture frames still rested on the table, photos intact. Janice and Harold Armstead with Newtown Beach's mayor. Harold with a local congressman. A younger Stephen posing next to a prize-weight marlin. Harold cutting the ribbon at a restaurant grand opening. Janice in Lycra pants and shirt untangling a sloop's halyard. Janice again, indoors on stage accepting an award. A recent photo of the Armsteads at the annual yacht club gala, sporting tuxes, gowns, and jewels.

Angie idly studied the last picture. The family looked rich, happy. Or maybe the platinum frame ringed with white crystals just made it appear that way.

"... impossible ... I couldn't move ... the knots ... tighter the more I tried ..."

Fragments of conversation reached Angie.

"... my wife ... right, Detective." Harold Armstead's voice now. Earnest sounding. "One knew his knots ... seaman probably ... don't know ... we aren't experienced sailors ..."

Bits of an Eminem song entered Angie's thoughts. Something about loving the way the other person lies. And Harold Armstead was lying. Angie was sure of it. Reversing direction, she moved back closer to the group.

"Poor Harold, he tried for ages to set me free," his wife was saying, "but the knots were just too tight."

Angie frowned. What the heck?

It was then that she noticed Stephen Armstead perched on the desk behind Grayson. The teenager had opened the Pirate Mike's box and was pulling out a paper tray filled with deep-fried squid.

The action took Angie back to when she was a child, sitting in Nona's kitchen watching her grandmother slicing calamari rings which she would later season, sauté and toss with linguini. As she watched Stephen Armstead eat his calamari, a second, more recent memory surfaced: that of an unfriendly van driver in a red hat.

Oh my God, Angie thought. I need to talk to Detective Grayson.

"Okay, Ms. Peretti. What's so important?"

Grayson and Angie were back in the foyer, the doors to the study closed.

"They did it."

"Who did what?"

"The Armsteads," Angie said impatiently. "They staged the burglary."

Grayson laughed in disbelief. "Why would they do that? Look at this place. They're rich."

Angie shook her head. "I don't think they are. At least not as rich as they were." She pantomimed opening a newspaper. "Did you see the article in the *Times* about the Mia Ristorante restaurant chain going bankrupt? There's a photo in the study showing Mr. Armstead cutting the ribbon at one of their grand openings. I think he either owns the chain or is a major investor. Maybe the Armsteads took a big financial hit and came up with a plan to claim the insurance payout while selling off the supposedly stolen goods. They'd make a mint."

"That's a pretty big jump, Ms. Peretti," Grayson chided gently. "Perhaps Armstead was in the picture because he's good friends with the restaurant owners."

His expression grew more dismissive when Angie told him about the Mia Ristorante van that had passed her on the street. "The driver probably was delivering food. No big clue there."

Angie bit back a snarky retort. "Mia Ristorante doesn't offer a delivery service, Detective," she said flatly. "Their restaurants use EveryEats, or a service like us." A sudden thought struck her. "Besides, where was the van coming from? The Armstead's house is the last one on the street. What if they hired that driver to haul off the supposedly stolen items?"

"Interesting theory," said Grayson, "but you have no proof. And the timing is tight. According to what you told my officers, you got here just after passing the van and found the Armsteads roped to chairs in the music room."

"But what if they weren't tied up? Or at least not all of them. What if my arrival surprised them? Maybe the sounds I heard were them rushing to tie everyone up. To make it seem like they were being held captive."

"It's more likely what you heard was the Armsteads trying to free themselves,"

Grayson suggested. "Mrs. Armstead said her husband worked hard to untie her."

Angie gave a stubborn shake of her head. "That's just it. She could have gotten free at any time."

Detective Grayson's eyebrows rose. "Explain."

Angie drummed her fingers on the entryway table, gathering her thoughts. "Mrs. Armstead said she was tied up so tight that she couldn't move, right?" Grayson nodded. "That was a lie. I saw the knots before your officers untied the ropes. Mr. Armstead and Stephen were bound tightly. But Mrs. Armstead's hands were secured with an easy release knot." She shot a questioning look at the detective. "Why would robbers—especially if they *were* seaman like Mr. Armstead said—use a knot anyone could escape from?"

Grayson commandeered the foyer chair and swept a hand through his graying blond hair. "Are you absolutely certain about that knot, Ms. Peretti. The Armsteads are very influential in this town. If I accuse them and you're wrong, my chief will kick my butt from here to the outer Channel Islands and back."

"I tied that knot every day at the marina," Angie said. "Two half hitches with a bend for quick release. To a layman it looks complicated. But it's dead simple. And you can release it with one hand." She held Grayson's gaze. "I'm telling you, Detective. Mrs. Armstead could have gotten free in seconds. And if her husband *had* tugged on that knot, it would have fallen apart."

Grayson rubbed his eyes tiredly. "Anything else, Ms. Peretti?"

Angie sank to the floor next to him, sighing as the coolness of the granite stone seeped through the thin denim of her jeans. She had been on the go since nine that morning. She was tired, sore, and hungry.

"Yeah. Mr. Armstead lied to you. If he and his wife aren't experienced sailors, why does he have a collection of books about rough water sailing?"

Grayson flashed the ghost of a jaunty grin. "Maybe me hearties aspire to sail the seven seas." Seeing Angie's pained expression, he sobered. "A couple named Lauders owned the house before the Armsteads. They sailed quite a bit. The books could have been here for years."

Angie stretched and yawned. "No, that can't be right," she said matter-of-factly. "Armstead said he was the one who had the study built. He made a big deal out of it. And one of the pictures in there shows Mrs. Armstead on a blue water racing boat."

Grayson sighed and heaved himself to his feet. "I missed that," he admitted. "Looks like I've got more questions for the Armsteads."

"Detective, one other thing," Angie said, scooting back to lean against the wall.

"It was Stephen that ordered the food from Pirate Mike's. How else did he know the delivery was an order of calamari?"

Grayson sketched a wordless acknowledgment before disappearing into the study.

Twenty minutes later, Grayson was back. Rousing herself from a half-doze, Angie saw him wave two newly arrived uniformed officers into the room.

"The Armsteads lawyered up," he said, walking over to her. "We'll be taking them downtown for more questioning."

"Can you charge them with anything?" Angie asked.

The detective spread his hands. "Filing a false police report. Conspiracy to commit fraud. Up to the D.A."

"What about failure to pay a promised delivery tip? I'm out 20 bucks."

The detective laughed sympathetically and helped Angie to her feet.

Sitting in her Prius a few minutes later, Angie watched as two uniformed officers led Janice and Harold Armstead to a squad car. She found herself grinning. The night had turned out okay. Sure, she had lost money. But she had done well. Detective Grayson had even said she might make a decent cop.

Pulling away from the curb, she turned left on Canal Street and headed for the bridge. Maybe she'd give that some thought. After all, crime was recession-proof. Catching crooks and delivering them to jail might be fun. She hit the switch to lower the driver's window. A fresh ocean breeze, carried on the rising tide, filled the car. Angie grinned again and began riffing on an old Bobby Fuller Four tune, belting out her take:

The Armsteads needed money 'cause they lost some
They tried to con the law and the law won
They're on their way to jail
And now my workday's done.

BACKSTORY

Ricky Sprague

There are people who are masters of what they do, and it's a real honor to see them in action. Like that guy who makes giant paintings of Jimi Hendrix while Jimi Hendrix music is playing. Or that guy who plays the Super Mario Bros sound effects on the violin while the game is going. Add to that list one Slip-N-Fall McCall, a grifter who worked a variety of low-level, under-the-radar kind of scams. His preferred wheeze was the slip-and-fall, whereby in which he would *slip and fall* in some public establishment, then threaten a lawsuit—at which point, hopefully, the ownership of the aforementioned establishment would settle such potential litigation out of court.

The spill he took in the Nic & Billy's dining room was a beaut. Even knowing who he was and what he did, there wasn't the slightest whiff of halibut. I had to admit that my heart stopped and I felt sympathetic pain as his feet shot out in front of him and he seemed to hang there, suspended in space, arranging his body for maximum drama with minimum pain.

When he hit the floor, it was with a magical thud.

His agony groans were subdued but affecting. He drew attention to the crack in the wood floor without being obvious. Adults cooed and crouched over him. Children cried. Slip was a capital-A Artist of the spill.

Also, he was a capital-D Dummy.

Maybe it was because he'd been out of town. Maybe it was hubris. Maybe it was laziness. Maybe he got caught up in the moment. But Slip had really "fallen down on the job," in a very literal sense, if he thought he was going to get away with these shenanigans in this particular family-friendly, themed restaurant.

I pushed my way through the crowd that had formed around him, leaned down over him and whispered, "Get up now, dude. Call it off."

He winced in such a way that it covered his winking at me. "Ooh, my back ..."

"Do you need a doctor?" someone asked, sympathetically.

"Can you move?" someone else asked, sympathetically.

"What goes on here?" another voice asked. Not sympathetically.

This voice belonged to a guy in skinny jeans and a manbun, who I recognized as one Geoffrey Tenpin. "Tenpin" wasn't his real last name, by the way. I don't know his real last name. "Tenpin" was a nickname he got when he beat a dude to death with a bowling pin. That was just one of a long list of violent credits. He wasn't one to be trifled with.

Slip-N-Fall resumed trifling with him: "Ow, ow, ow, my back is *so* hurt. I think I've slipped a disk and cracked something ..."

"Well, don't move. Me and the boys'll help you to the back."

"The boys" were a couple of other dudes that I also recognized as torpedoes. Now at this point you're probably wondering why there'd be three torpedoes working at Nic & Billy's, home of Family Nite Thursday and Funday Brunch. The answer ties into the reason why I was so anxious for Slip to just scrap this whole thing, stand up and pay the full tab and get right out of there as quickly as possible.

One of the owners of the six Nic & Billy's Southern California franchises was Quick Vandyke.

Yeah. *That* Quick Vandyke.

Sensing that things were perhaps spiraling out of control, I attempted to calm the situation: "Maybe we all oughtta just take a few deep breaths and count to ten and let Mr. McCall here consider just how hurt he really is."

Geoffrey smiled at me. "He says he's hurt. You think he's not?"

"I'm hurt pretty bad, Dan," Slip said to me in a "why-you-gotta-be-such-a-killjoy?" kind of tone that was ironic, considering I was trying to save his life.

"My boss is on his way," Geoffrey said ominously. A maintenance guy or something brought out this canvas stretcher, and the other torpedoes rolled Slip-N-Fall onto it. They weren't very delicate with him. Almost like they didn't believe he was actually injured, but were willing to make his "injuries" a reality if he trifled with them.

"I'm sure we can work something out," Slip said. He still didn't get the trouble he was in.

"We'll go back with you," I said. I glanced around, expecting to see at least some other members of our party backing me up. However, as it turned out, Meggie, Kandall Frye, Iggie the Lamppost, L-Train, and Dr. Crack (not a medical doctor), had all scrammed out.

"You sure about that?" Geoffrey asked.

"Yeah," I said with resolution that sounded pretty authentic, probably.

To the rest of the guests Geoffrey said, "Everyone relax. Things are fine here; we're just gonna take this dude into the office so he can rest his back."

We went past the kitchen to a large office in the back. The two other torpedoes took Slip to the leather couch on the far side of the room and tilted the stretcher so that Slip tumbled onto it.

"Wait here," Geoffrey said as they left.

"Those were rough dudes," Slip said, sitting up. It was the most insightful thing he'd said in a while. "Not the types I'd expect to be working at a local chain of family restaurants."

"You know this place is owned by Quick Vandyke, right?" I said.

His face sagged for a few seconds. Then he chuckled in a very unconvincing way and he said, "Naw. This place is owned by some LLC or something. It's a faceless corporation."

"Quick Vandyke is one of the faces that owns that LLC."

He leaned forward and whispered, "But Quick Vandyke is a *gangster*."

The door opened. Quick Vandyke stood in the doorway, with a judgmental look on his face. "I've always been a legitimate businessman. Now, however, I'm even *more* legitimate."

Like Geoffrey Tenpin, Quick Vandyke's last name wasn't the one he was born with. It was a nickname based on the arrangement of his facial hair. Also, his first name wasn't actually "Quick." That, too, was a nickname. Referencing how quick he was to kill people who crossed him.

In the past, that is. Now that he was *more* legitimate than ever, he was beyond straight-up murder. I hoped.

He wagged his finger at me, like I'd made a naughty. "I thought you had more sense," he said.

That wasn't something I heard very often. Especially from someone of his stature. So I admit it inflated my ego a bit.

"You, on the other hand, are not very smart." This was directed at Slip. "I'm going to give you some friendly advice, *Slip-N-Fall McCall.* If you plan on starting any kind of litigation or claim against me or my business, you will experience a great deal of physical pain. *Real* physical pain, not this staged stuff you tried to pull tonight."

"That's more a warning than advice," I pointed out.

"It's an iron-clad prediction of the future."

"I actually feel a lot better." To demonstrate, Slip started sort of twisting his body back and forth and thrusting his pelvis, like he was in a 1980s jazzercise video.

Quick Vandyke smiled. "Get a load of you. Speedy recovery."

"Mr. Vandyke, I appreciate you being so decent about this little misunderstanding."

"That's all it was," Slip added. "A misunderstanding."

"Communication is the key to life," Quick said. "Clears up so many things before they fester into dangerous wounds that can't be healed. If you get my meaning."

"We both get your meaning," I spoke for myself and Slip, who still hadn't stopped back-and-forth twisting.

Quick slapped us both on the back. "Tell you what. To show there's no hard feelings, I'm gonna give each of you a book of coupons, good for one free appetizer a week for the next six weeks."

"Thanks!" I said.

Slip looked disappointed he wasn't at least getting the meal comped. Of course, he wasn't looking at the big picture. Namely, that Quick Vandyke was the type of person who—in the past—might very well kill someone if they tried to scam him the way Slip had tried tonight.

This would be a good place to end the story. And I wish I could, it coming in under 1,500 words so far. Alas. The story took a couple more twists, the way a story sometimes does when it's trying to prove it hasn't hurt its back. That previous sentence didn't make a lot of sense but I've never been very good with similes.

Three nights later, Wednesday, the little slip-and-fall incident at Nic & Billy's had left my brains.

As I got to the door of my apartment around ten-thirty I heard sounds coming from inside. This was disappointing. My roommate, Chris, was supposed to be working late at a screening or something, and I was looking forward to some uninterrupted video game time in the living room. With so much stress in the world, a person needs time to decompress.

Opening the door, I noticed the lights were out. It wasn't like Chris to move around in the dark. He's not exactly the most crepuscular kind of guy, if you know what I mean.

Unless he was having sexytime. Dude—was he having sexytime? It would be out of character for him to have it in the living room, but maybe he was with someone "adventurous." Good for him!

I announced myself, then discreetly added: "I'm just gonna keep my head down and go to my room."

Something fell over, then something bigger fell over, then there was the sound of groaning. At this point I couldn't help it. I looked. Only one figure. I turned on the light and there was Slip, rolling around on the floor in the space between the kitchen and living room.

"You're not trying that slip-and-fall stuff on me, are you, Slip?"

He struggled to get up. He'd obviously taken a bad, nonprofessional spill. Also, his left arm was in a sling. He wore a back brace, and a cervical collar. His right eye was swollen and black and his left cheek bruised.

He said woozily, "Who are you? Do I know you? Why are you in my apartment?"

Now I admit I'm not the most observant dude in the world, but even *I've* never mistaken my own apartment for Slip's. When he was in town, Slip lived in one of those buildings that sort of looks like a motel, with the doors facing out toward the parking lot, you know? It's over in the Beverlywood area. My own apartment is a pretty nice enclosed building with parking underneath.

Nevertheless, I looked around the room before answering him. Sure enough, Chris's toys—excuse me, his collectable action figures—were all over the walls. Some were on the ground, actually. Come to think of it, the place looked in disarray, in a very literal sense.

"Were you tossing my apartment?"

"This is *my* apartment, and I don't know who you are." Slip made a movement as if to go around me. "I'm getting out of here and calling the police!"

I grabbed his right arm, and he grimaced and groaned. "Sorry. Slip. This is *my* apartment. Do you have amnesia or something?"

"That's it, Dan!" he said, his face sort of arranging into a bruised smile. "I've got amnesia. I had a bad accident a couple days ago."

"It does look bad. A lot worse than it did when I saw you last."

He nodded with his whole body, because the cervical collar limited his range of neck motion. "I got conked on the noggin and it gave me anesthesia."

"You mean amnesia?"

"Yeah. See, Dan? I can't even remember the word for what I got." He smiled smugly.

"That was pretty good, the way you 'forgot' the word for 'amnesia.' But something just occurred to me—you called me Dan just then, and you called me Dan earlier too. But I didn't tell you my name—so how could you remember it, if you've got amnesia?"

"The answer to your question is, that I noticed your name when I was looking around your apartment ...”

"But you just said you thought it was *your* apartment.”

His face sagged as much as it could in the circumstances. "Brain injuries are weird! And I didn't exactly start off with a full deck!”

"You have a point.”

"You're in *cahoots*! You're an informant! A snitch! A narc!”

"I'm not any of those things! Slip—what's this about?”

"Do you deny that you work with the po-po?”

"I have on occasion had to work with the police—totally against my will. To bring killers to justice, you know ...” It sounded like lame rationalization when I said it.

"Ah-*ha*!" He tried to lift his left arm triumphantly. Instead he just winced and whimpered.

"Sit on the couch and tell me about it.”

He sat down with a wheeze. "Be honest, Dan. Did you conspire with the FBI to get me to re-open my slip-and-fall case against Nic & Billy's?”

"I can't even wrap my head around how dumb that sounds. No. I didn't do anything like that.”

"I *knew* they were just using mental psychology on me.”

"Who?”

He gave me this sort of wholehearted look that made my soul ache. "I'm sorry I doubted you, Dan.”

"It's okay.”

"You're a good friend.”

"You are too.”

He whined. "And I repay your friendship by breaking into your apartment to look for evidence that you were working with the feds so I can give it to Quick Vandyke so he'll kill you for me.”

"I retract my previous statement.”

"I'm sorry, Dan!" He leaned forward so his head was on my shoulder and moved his body like he was crying with remorse.

"Tell me what happened.”

"The morning after I tried my slip-and-fall gag at Nic & Billy's, there's this knock on my door. I go to answer it and there's this dudebro standing there, he shows me this FBI badge and he says his name is Ross Dover. He says he knows all about my slip-and-fall accident and he wants to ensure I file a complaint, get a lawyer, and so on.

"I told him, no, it was a misunderstanding and so on. He says, no, the misunderstanding is that I'm *not* going to file the complaint and sue and so on. I tell him, no, the misunderstanding was that I slipped in the first place. He says, no, I'm not listening, I need to clear up the nature of the misunderstanding, it's not that I fell, it's that I decided not to do my civic duty and file a complaint, and I tell him that the misunderstanding, the only misunderstanding, was that I fell in the first place, because that was actually *my* fault, my shoes need re-soling and so on. He says that I have a dangerous misunderstanding of the current situation if I think that's where the misunderstanding is ..."

"Slip, I'm more a big-picture kind of guy, if you know what I mean."

"Right. Anyway, he says that he's part of some federal task force that's been after Quick Vandyke for years, but they've never been able to get anything on him. They want a way to start going after him with these different, like, oh, what'd he call them ... not institutions ... these like, you know what I mean? These sort of ... I can't think of the word ..."

"Maybe it's your amnesia?"

"Anyway, he tells me that he's already working with *you,* and you've agreed to testify that when I slipped and fell, he and his torpedoes beat me up really bad to get me to shut up about it. So I'm supposed to file a complaint on the slip-and-fall, then file something about him beating me up—*regulatory agencies*!"

"Huh? Oh—that's what you were trying to think of?"

"Right. Anyway, he tells me that you—you know, since you've worked with the cops before—and you have to admit, you *have* worked with cops before, Dan ..." he said it accusingly.

"Yeah, I'm not proud of it, let's move on with the story."

"... He says that you're working with him to bring down Quick Vandyke, and you gave him my address and so on."

"That's not true."

"I know that now. He was using mental psychology on me, to manipulate me."

"Did this Dover dude beat you up?"

Slip nodded as best he could, in the circumstances. "He told me that the story would be that Quick Vandyke took us into the back of Nic & Billy's, and he said, if I was going to slip and fall, I needed to do a really bang-up job of it. By which he meant that Quick Vandyke and his torpedoes would throw me down the stairs that go into the basement at the restaurant, you know? I said, okay, whatever, just to get rid of him at this point, I tell him I'll swear to anything. But he says, no, we have to really be able to sell it, because I wasn't injured enough, and the injuries had to be real, attested to by a real doctor. So Dover threw me down the stairs a couple of times."

"Wait. This FBI guy threw you down the stairs at your apartment?"

"It was only the fact that I'm such a practiced slip-and-fall expert that I was able to avoid dying, but, dangit, look what he did to me!"

"This Dover dude messed you up pretty good."

"Took me to this doctor in Van Nuys—a real shady cat. I think he was a fed too. Or at least, fed-friendly. Then, Dover had me sign a statement, saying it was Quick Vandyke who beat me up. Then he discharged me and said that he'd be in touch when he needed me and I should lay low awhile and so on."

"Well, I didn't tell him about what happened. So how'd he know about it?"

"I think he might've been there that night. When he was driving me to the doctor he mentioned something about me and my Long Island Mojito-chugging friends doing something positive for the world for a change."

"Izzie won our Long Island Mojito-chug-a-lug that night."

"She cheated, by the way."

"No such thing, Slip."

"What do we do?"

"Well, your idea of going to Quick Vandyke has some merit. He should know you're being pulled into this against your will. Maybe he can even help."

"If it was up to Slip, the whole thing would've been dropped, just like we agreed," I explained to Quick Vandyke at his legitimate business home office on Sunset. I said this in what I believed to be a highly persuasive way, in a very literal sense. "But, he was coerced into filing that assault report by this rogue federal agent." It seemed an especially compelling touch to throw the word "rogue" in there, as this agent was behaving very badly.

Quick Vandyke did that thing where you put your hands together sort of like you're praying, and then put your index fingers up against your pursed lips, to indicate just how much thought he was giving the situation. I was certain he'd say something along the lines of, *"I'm not unreasonable. I understand that Slip is in a difficult position. No hard feelings and to the extent that anything further needs to be done, I will take care of it from here."*

He sighed. "I'm not unreasonable," he began. I felt a wave of relief wash over me.

"I understand that Slip is in a difficult position." At this point, I started to think it was just entirely possible that Quick Vandyke might offer to pay for Slip to get a new couch or something, and maybe throw in a Nintendo Switch for me.

Then, he went on:

"But the fact is your idiot friend tried to pull a slip-and-fall in *my* establishment, and this 'rogue' federal agent as you put it—" (he said it what seemed to me an unnecessarily sneering way) "—is now trying to use it to get at me in this convoluted, roundabout way that's giving me a headache."

"Slip's in a lot of pain too."

"I want you to make it all go away."

"I can get you an aspirin."

"I mean, I want you to get Dover to lay off me."

"Isn't that more your line?"

"In the past. But not now. I'm a clean-hands kinda guy."

"So am I. In fact, *my* clean-hands policy is a lot more long-standing-er than yours."

He waved his hand in a way that I wasn't sure if he was trying to shut me up or getting ready to hit me, or both. "Shut up," he said, without hitting me. "Agent Dover is a pest. He joined this task force just as I was moving all of my interests into fully legitimate businesses. He sees me as his one that got away, I guess. Now he's just desperate. I'm almost embarrassed for him."

He rose from his chair and went to the safe that stood in the corner of the room behind his desk. From the safe he pulled out some papers, flipped through them, and handed one of them to me. "This is everything I've got on Agent Ross Dover."

"Why are you giving me this?" I asked nervously.

"You're going to do me a great favor. I don't want to hear how you do it or any other details. But you're going to get rid of this problem for me."

"I'm not—"

"Don't say anything else! I don't want to hear anything about it. I'm a legitimate businessman. Having said that, I expect you to clear this up for me by the end of the week. I do not want to be charged with assault, and I definitely don't want any health inspectors or some other bureaucrats going after my businesses."

I scanned the paper before laying it on the desk. "There's no reason for me to know this guy's address, birthday, his wife's name, her job, or whatever else is on there ..."

"This *rogue federal agent* nearly killed your friend. He poisoned your relationship with him. He used mental psychology on him to convince him that you'd betrayed him. This man won't let me leave the past in the past, so I can get on with providing families with wholesome entertainment and good food at reasonable prices."

"Those Spicy Cheddar Onion Rings *are* pretty good."

He smiled. "You do this for me, and you can have one free meal a week for the next year. Including from the Steak 'N' Seafood page."

"I usually skip that one. Too pricy."

"Going forward the entire menu will be open for you."

"So what am I supposed to do?"

"I don't know. But if your friend files any complaints against me, I will make it very difficult for him. Whether he was coerced into it or not. Do you understand?"

I understood.

I also started to get really resentful. Quick Vandyke had a point about this Dover dude poisoning my relationship with Slip. That annoyed me. He also had a point about Dover beating up Slip. That was pretty rotten too.

But how was that my responsibility? I mean, obviously it was my responsibility because Quick Vandyke made it my responsibility. Still, I didn't understand how it was my responsibility. Moreover, I didn't *want* the responsibility. I'm literally irresponsible.

I took the Dover information back to my apartment and showed it to Slip. Sure enough, the image on the page was of the man who'd beaten Slip.

"You gonna kill him, Dan?"

"Why does everyone think I go around killing people?"

"It's a sort of vibe you give off."

"Well, I'm not a killer."

"What *are* you gonna do?"

"I could write him a note and leave it in his mailbox."

"I doubt that'd do anything."

"I could order a bunch of pizzas and have them sent to his house."

"That's kind of funny. But I don't think it'd be very effective at getting him to leave me and Quick Vandyke alone."

We spent a lot of time spitballing. Most of what we came up with wasn't as good as the stuff I mentioned above.

Finally, after what seemed like literally forever, I had a real brainstorm: "What if I slipped and fell on *his* property?"

Slip's face lit up, as much as it could being so bruised. "You mean—then *you* could sue *him*?"

"Exactly!"

"That's poetic justice!"

"My favorite kind of justice."

"I can even teach you to fall like a professional."

I'll be honest. At the beginning, Slip and I were both fairly enthusiastic about my plan for poetic justice. But after spending about twenty minutes practicing falling, we were fanatical about it, in a very literal sense. It felt like a can't-miss slam-dunk, or a can't-miss slip-and-fall, if you will, so to speak.

Like so many of the best plans, it was simple: I'd walk up to his front door, knock, and pretend to advocate on behalf of some important issue or something. Then, as I was leaving, I'd slip and fall on his porch, sprawling on the front walk, injuring my back. Ipso facto, I'd threaten to sue him—then drop the suit if he agreed to leave Slip alone.

It was fool-proof.

The one concern that I had was that I needed to ensure I had a witness. To that end, I attempted to corral my roommate Chris. I won't sully this story with his response. Instead I'll skip straight to Bay-Zo, who enthusiastically agreed to "just happen to be walking by" when I took my spill. He also suggested we try to extort maybe fifteen-hundred out of Dover, which would work out to five-hundred apiece.

At first it seemed like overkill but on further consideration it was more poetic justice. A good lesson for Dover, and a little extra scratch for us. Truly, three brains were better than two, when it came to caper-planning.

Time being of the essence, we decided to do it around 7:30 the next night. At the very least, someone should be home around that time. Federal agents do mostly office work anyway and keep pretty regular hours. His wife did something with billing or something at an insurance company, so it seemed reasonable she'd be home.

The next night, parked around the corner from the house, the plan seemed somehow less fool-proof.

At 7:33, Bay-Zo sent me a text: *Ten mins out.*

At 7:44, I decided I needed to start walking to the house. It got to be too late, then my story that I was going around advocating for some cause might get suspicious.

This was when I realized something all three of us had overlooked: If Agent Dover starts asking around to his neighbors "Hey, did this good-looking dude go to your house advocating for this important cause on the night he slipped and fell on our porch?" and all his neighbors tell him, "No, he never did," then it's going to look really suspicious.

At this time, which was 8:01, I got another text from Bay-Zo: *Be there in 10.*

This was kind of a relief, because it gave me a chance to go knock on a couple of other doors first, before I went straight up to Agent Dover's house.

I went up to the house on the corner.

At my knock, a woman answered. Her expression went from annoyed to pleased as she looked me over. This is literally true, I'm not just saying it. And, I was quite pleased to see her. She gave off this sort of frustrated-lonely-housewife-just-back-from-spin-class kinda vibe. Maybe after I was done with my slip-and-fall bit I could come back to this house and ask her out.

I got another text from Bay-Zo. *s/b 10 more mins.*

So I had time to chat. "Hello," I said.

"Hi."

"I'm going door-to-door about a very serious issue." I hadn't yet practiced this part of it because I wanted it to be spontaneous and fresh. Usually I work a lot better "in the moment," so to speak, in a very literal sense. However, I was starting to realize that might not have been the best modus operandi in this case.

"What issue is that?"

"Tort reform."

"Seriously?"

"Yeah. Tort reform is a very serious problem." I had to admit, for an extemporaneous conversation I was really killing it. Sometimes my brain really comes through.

"Are you *against* tort reform?"

And just like that, with one question, my enthusiasm plunged, literally. "Well, I mean, it's a complicated process, as I'm sure you know."

I admit I was starting to feel that I should have picked a topic I knew something about, and not some phrase that I think Chris had used when he was denying my request to help me out with this plan. "As I said, it's complicated. Right now, I'm trying to gauge interest."

"In tort reform?"

"Yes. Can I put you down as a yes?"

"Yes to what? Tort reform?"

"Yes. Correct."

"This is bizarre. Is this a joke, or something?"

"Tort reform isn't a joke."

"I guess that's true." She got this sort of contemplative look on her face. "It's really funny—I was just sitting here thinking how much I'd like some company right now, you know? Would you like to come inside?"

I got another text from Bay-Zo. *Ten mins out!*

"Well, as long as you need some company …"

At this point I decided that I should probably abandon Plan A, and go straight to Plan B, which involved me spending time with a lonely housewife who, if I wasn't mistaken, was interested in me in a carnal way. Unfortunately I wasn't sure that this Plan B would in any way help to get Agent Dover to lay off Slip and, by extension, Quick Vandyke. Which would probably mean coming up with a Plan C. To be honest, I'd already started to doubt the potential for success of Plan A, anyway.

Slip would understand, and Bay-Zo (who, come to think of it, wasn't the most responsible dude) had been ten minutes out for about an hour by then.

As she closed the door behind us she said, "You're very healthy-looking."

Then she said something else, but I couldn't hear it over the incredibly loud crashing noise that starting ringing inside my skull. Then everything went completely dark.

When I started coming awake I heard a voice saying, "I couldn't just let him *leave.*"

"Yes, you could," said another voice.

The voices seemed to be coming from very far away, down a long tunnel filled with marbles. Marbles that were pounding against my skull, which was throbbing with pain.

"That would have been like spurning a gift."

"What if one of the neighbors saw him?"

"Nobody's going to find his body anyway."

"He just got another text. 'Ten mins out,' it says. Somebody knows where he is! He probably knows who *we* are!"

"He's too dumb—"

"*Nobody's* that dumb!"

"That tort reform thing was pretty suspect." Now I was awake enough to recognize the woman's voice. The woman I'd been about to make sexy time with.

"You have no impulse control." This must have been the dude who conked me on the noggin.

She laughed. "Neither of us do—and *you love it!*"

He laughed. "Yeah, I really do. Still, we've got to take care of this guy."

"Let's just take him to the basement and cut his throat. Stick him in the freezer."

"Probably best. Look at him. He's a decent specimen."

"When I saw him, I got pretty worked up."

"You did, huh?"

"I wanted to set him up for you ..."

It seemed a safe assumption they were talking about me. But it didn't seem a good idea to ask them, to verify.

There were sounds of grunting and squeaking furniture.

I slowly opened one eye and saw them going at it on the couch.

Carefully, slowly, while they were both facing toward the other wall, I rolled over and crept out of the room. Once out, I tiptoed through the foyer to the front door. There was something funny about that door. I couldn't open it. It required a key, from the inside. Huh.

"Leaving so soon?" the guy said.

He was kind of wiry, wearing only underwear, and holding that sap like he really knew how to use it. Ordinarily I probably wouldn't have been very impressed, but his eyes had a look of insane determination. In a way I kind of admired it—he had a goal.

I had another brainstorm: "I work with the po-po a lot. I'm working with Special Agent Dover of the FBI. We're doing an undercover operation to catch you two—"

He laughed, sort of mocking. "That jackass has lived down the street from us for four years—and he never even realized it!"

"Oh, he *realized it,*" I said, acting. "He just *pretended* to be a jackass."

"Then I guess he'll be coming in, right?"

"Any minute."

We stood for a few seconds. I said, "I'll just be going now—"

"You have no idea who we are, do you?"

"Of course I do. We all do. Me and Dover and—"

"Who are we then?" he asked in this really snotty tone.

"You're killers. Who are about to get caught, at any time now—"

"He just got another text," the woman said, carrying my phone into the foyer. She looked fetching in her shorty robe. "Bay-Zo is ten minutes out."

"That's code for 'We're going to break down the door—' "

"He's got no idea who we are."

He puffed out his chest. "My wife and I are the Pisces Slayer."

"Exactly. We know. And now your reign of terror—"

"That name doesn't mean anything to him," the wife said.

The husband sort of wilted a little. "You haven't heard of the *Pisces Slayer*? There have been seven cable shows about us!"

"Eight," his wife corrected.

"Eight?"

"You keep forgetting that episode of *Forensics Forever*!"

"No—I remembered that one!"

"I saw that," I chimed in. "It was pretty interesting."

"Thanks. They got a lot of stuff wrong. For one thing, there's *two of us*, obviously. Nobody knows that."

"And no one's ever going to know that either," the wife said.

"I won't tell anyone," I assured them.

"I thought everyone already knew about us?"

"They do. You just hit me pretty hard." I took a page from Slip: "Brain injuries are weird!"

"Let's just get this over with," the guy said. He started stalking toward me in this kind of crouch position. I thought he was going to sort of toy with me, moving around in this intimidating way, but instead he made a movement that was so quick I'm not sure I actually even saw it.

I think he expected me to be quicker on my feet, or to try to fight back, or something.

Yet in this moment, I once again thought of Slip, and our original plan.

When I fell down and backward, Slip-N-Fall McCall style, this Pisces guy's momentum carried him forward and over me. My foot, in the air in front of me, connected with his chin, and his head snapped backward with a startling sound.

His body sort of crumpled to the floor.

The wife made her own movement toward me. She was fast. Instead of trying to get up I kicked my leg out and slammed into her knee.

She let out a shriek like nothing I'd ever heard before.

While she rolled and moaned around on the floor, I got the keys from the husband's unconscious body, unlocked the door, and ran to the neighbor's house. Not Special Agent Dover's house. That dude had too many strikes against him, what with trying to force Slip to do undercover work for him, and living down the block from married serial killers for four years without realizing it.

Special Agent Dover tried to take over as soon as the Los Angeles Sheriff's deputies arrived. Then, Dover's boss showed up. His name was Pine. He seemed pretty competent. I talked to him for a few minutes.

The conversation was interrupted by a text from Bay-Zo: *Here. Why cops? Turning back.*

I replied: *Over now. Talk later. Thx.*

Then Pine went away for a few minutes. From where I was standing on the sidewalk I could see him talking to Dover. Dover didn't look happy.

Pine came back. He said, "Special Agent Dover has explained the *unorthodox* turn his investigation into Quick Vandyke has recently taken."

"You mean, beating up Slip and trying to frame Quick Vandyke for the crime?"

"Let's set that aside. Right now we have another concern. Said concern involves you managing to snag a couple of notorious serial killers who happened to be living next to an FBI Special Agent without his knowledge."

"He was too busy throwing people down stairs to 'force' them to 'cooperate' with him."

"Don't be snarky. You're about to win. Special Agent Dover will release your friend the slip-and-fall guy from his obligations to his country, if you will agree to keep your mouth shut about what transpired here tonight."

"You're going to give Dover credit for catching them?"

"And for saving your life after they knocked you unconscious and abducted you. We think it's better than your whole door-to-door-tort-reform-slip-and-fall thing, you know?"

"Maybe."

"Think about it. You get what you came for, Special Agent Dover gets some publicity, and the FBI gets a nice boost in the public's mind."

I considered this for a few seconds. "All right. I'll agree to it. But I also want ... ten thousand bucks." After everything that had happened, between Slip getting beaten up, me getting knocked out, and Bay-Zo having to deal with traffic, I figured we'd earned a little extra than what we'd planned.

Pine laughed.

Bay-Zo got his five hundred. I gave five grand to Slip, since he'd been beaten pretty bad. The rest I gave to Chris to pay some back rent I "owed" him.

The whole thing felt sort of anticlimactic, somehow. Maybe it was because I'd actually accomplished what I'd set out to do. It was an unfamiliar feeling.

I got another "unfamiliar" feeling watching the *Forensics Forever* episode about the capture of the Pisces Slayer. The official story was obviously nothing like what actually happened. Plus, the guy who played me in the re-enactments was a real doofus.

It's hard to know who to trust these days.

BURGLAR'S BUNGLE

A You-Solve-It by Guy Belleranti

S heriff Hugo Melch brought the car to a siren screaming stop outside his aunt's ranch style house in the Copper City foothills.

"It's beautiful out here, Sheriff," Deputy Sprott said as he slid his lanky body out of the car. "Bet your Aunt Molly has great Copper City views at night."

"Yeah, but having your nearest neighbor over a mile away isn't safe for a lone woman."

Aunt Molly swung open the front door and led them to her bedroom in the rear of the house.

"There!" she cried, pointing at the open window along the foot of her bed. "That's where the burglar came in."

Melch stomped across the room and kneeled on the bed, its springs creaking under his bulk as he looked out the window. The window's screen lay on the sunbaked ground, but he saw no legible footprints. He examined the window. "No sign of forced entry. No scratches or marks." He swung around. "Auntie, you should keep your windows locked."

"I do, and it was!" Aunt Molly snapped. "I checked every window yesterday afternoon right after Chrissy and Herman left."

"What were *they* doing here?"

"Your anti-social self may not understand it, Hugo, but I love having my daughter stop by with her friends. However, their visit yesterday wasn't just a social call. I'd hired Herman to install new extra strong locks on the front and back doors like you'd suggested"

"Nice," Melch said, "but that doesn't do much good if a window's unlocked."

Aunt Molly glared at him. "Didn't you hear me, Hugo? All my windows were locked. I figured it made no sense paying good dough for good door locks if a window was unlocked."

Melch scowled. "Okay. Sprott, let's check the other windows."

"Well?" Aunt Molly asked when they rejoined her five minutes later in the bedroom.

"All locked tight," Melch admitted. He pursed his lips. "So, Auntie, you said on the phone your jewelry was taken. Anything else missing?"

Aunt Molly sniffled. "Afraid so, Hugo. Your late Uncle Gene's rare coin collection was swiped from that antique bookcase in the living room."

"The dirty thief!" Sprott said.

"That he certainly is," said Aunt Molly. "But how'd he open this window without leaving any marks?"

"Good question," Sprott said. "You got any ideas, Sheriff?"

"Yep." Melch turned to his aunt. "Auntie, who's visited you since Chrissy and Herman left yesterday?"

"Hardly anyone. Just Dinah and Chrissy earlier today."

"Dinah?"

"You've met her before, Hugo. She and her husband live in that house a mile or so before mine."

"Hmm." Melch unwrapped a piece of gum, stuffed it into his mouth and chewed slowly. "What time were Chrissy and Dinah here?"

"Each arrived around ten. We had a lovely Saturday brunch. They left about 12:30 and I headed into town for my mystery readers meeting at the library. I returned three hours later, came in here to put away the necklace I'd worn for the brunch and meeting, saw the open window and discovered my jewelry box was gone."

Melch stopped chewing. "Three hours. ... That's plenty of time."

"Plenty of time for what, Sheriff?" asked Sprott.

"Plenty of time for either Chrissy or Dinah to return and come in the window she had unlocked during brunch."

Aunt Molly's face whitened. "You can't believe one of them ..." She sank onto the bed.

Melch averted his eyes. Too bad he couldn't pass the investigation over to Sprott. But as top cop his job was to follow where the clues led. He was trying to think up a good reply to his aunt when a voice called from the front of the house.

"Yoo-hoo. Molly, I just saw your text about the burglary. I'm here to give you a supporting hug!"

"That's Dinah!" Aunt Molly rushed from the room.

"You texted her?" Melch asked, following on her heels.

"Yes, Hugo. And Chrissy too."

A long-legged woman turned from her examination of the front door. "Nice new locks, Molly. Obviously your burglar didn't come in this way."

"No. He came in a window."

"Dear me. Let me give you my promised hug."

Melch waited, then finally cleared his throat.

"Ah, hello, Hugo ... Deputy Sprott," Dinah said. "Have you found any—"

The doorbell cut her short.

Aunt Molly pulled open the door and Chrissy burst in, with Herman right behind. "Oh, Mom! I read your text. How horrible! I decided I better come right away. Then I saw Herman pulling up in front of my apartment, so we came together."

Herman shifted from one foot to the other. "I'm awfully sorry, Molly. I was sure those locks would make things safer for you. They were supposed to be burglar proof!"

"Oh, Herman, it's not your fault. The creep didn't come in a door."

"Oh, but then how—"

"Your mom says he came in a window," Dinah said.

"A *locked* window," Aunt Molly corrected.

"You mean the burglar broke the glass?" Chrissy asked. "If so, I bet Herman can fix it."

"Sure," Herman said. "That's a specialty of mine."

"The glass wasn't broken," Melch said. "And the window wasn't locked. Someone had unlocked it."

"Hugo—"

"Sorry, Auntie, but I have a job to do." Melch looked around the room studying the faces. Cousin Chrissy, Herman, Dinah, Aunt Molly and Sprott. "It's nice to have everyone gathered together," he said.

"Well, we all care about Molly," Dinah said.

"Is that so?"

"Hugo, please—"

"Auntie, *let me do my job*."

Someone sucked in a breath, and a sudden tension filled the air.

"The window the burglar opened *was* locked yesterday," Melch went on. "However, earlier today someone unlocked it. Anyone want to confess?"

No one said a word.

"Last chance," Melch said, looking again from face to face. Then, he shot out his right arm. "You were here today for brunch!"

"Uh, y-yes," Dinah stammered, "but that doesn't mean ..."

Melch shot out the arm again. "You were also at the brunch."

Chrissy gasped, and cried, "Hugo, I'm your cousin!"

"That doesn't make you innocent."

"I-I went home, did laundry and cleaned. I didn't unlock any window."

"Of course you didn't," Herman said, squeezing Chrissy's hand. "Sheriff, like Dinah said, we all care about Molly. Accusing any of us is unfair. Perhaps Molly opened the window to let some fresh air into her bedroom last night and forgot to close it. I've done that at my place and I bet you have too."

"Is that what happened, Auntie?" Melch asked.

"Well, I sometimes do open windows to air things out, but I didn't last night," Aunt Molly said. "However, Herman's right. What you're doing is unfair, mean, unprofessional and—"

"Effective!" Melch finished.

"How is it effective?" Dinah snapped. "I didn't open a window, and I believe Chrissy when she says she didn't. Berating innocent people won't help you accomplish anything."

"But I have accomplished something," Melch said, smiling. "I riled people until the burglar bungled an almost perfect crime by making a slip of the lip."

Who is the burglar?

Solution in next month's issue ...

Solution to May's You-Solve-It

Pocket Change by John M. Floyd

The headlights of the car in the driveway. If Linda Bell has really been staring straight ahead into those headlights the whole time, there's no way she could've identified the car's make and model.

Made in United States
North Haven, CT
03 June 2022

19835047R00046